SILVER BELLS
—A Christmas Horror Story—

Sandy Lender

Foreword by Steven L. Shrewsbury

2

Dedication

For Christine

Because all BFF stories have threads of you
woven in them somewhere.

Foreword

Christmas and horror stories, well, I'm sure we all have some of those from family gatherings over the years, but I digress. I'd have not thought the two would go together in fiction, aside from past horror films that have taken a, ahem, stab at it like *Violent Night* and others, but perhaps the timing is right for such a tale.

Sandy Lender's *Silver Bells* is such a yarn, and right for the time.

While weaving an interesting tale, Sandy never fails to paint out the holiday scenery around these fascinating characters and plot. While not as grim as the film I mentioned above, her voice chronicles a story that is a tad disturbing and fascinating at the same time. Known more for her fantasy work, Sandy grabs the quiet horror plate by the edges and sends it across the room. The realism is what struck me, probably because it reminded me of Christmas activities and things that go in in town at such a time.

However, it wasn't just the sets and X-Mas stuff in the framework, but the people within. Her characters (the lead Ivy especially) breathe and come off as genuine folks. When turmoil develops, even on a small scale, one wants to see what happens next.

The rollicking dialogue from these tangible characters draws one in quick. The desire to give a damn grips the reader well, and I found myself curious what would happen to each of the individuals. Sandy controls tension like a chiropractor. Her

4

diligence to detail is near to mind boggling not just for the seasonal setting but the action and some violence. Sometimes the actual horror in life isn't from a four-legged monster but from the things we fear within.

For an entertaining read in a Christmas setting, *Silver Bells* delivers and will make one want to seek out more of Sandy Lender's fiction.

Steven L. Shrewsbury
Author of *Reckoning Day, Bladespell,* and more

Introduction

Something about a December 25th deadline each year reminds me of running a marathon. I live about half a continent away from my family and core friend group, so I typically rush to acquire the special gifts that I think loved ones will be most excited to receive, wrap these treasures, package them carefully for mailing, and ship them so the U.S. Postal Service has time to misdirect-and-redirect while still delivering gifts in time for Santa's Big Day.

I've had many a year with choir practice and handbell-sequence memorization until the night of a Christmas concert, which many churches are holding prior to Christmas Day as of late. Baking cookies and pies is something I enjoy, but I must know the schedules of neighbors and nearby friends before putting myself through the deadline anxiety.

And the cards. The cards must go out early enough for messed-up addresses to be returned, re-addressed, and re-sent.

All this to say, Christmas makes a perfect analogy for a marathon. Thus, when it was time for the 2023 International Three-Day Novel Contest, which is a seventy-two-hour writing marathon extraordinaire, my brain said, "Write your marathon novel about Christmas. And make it stressful."

For seventy-two hours over that Labor Day Weekend, I typed out the story of Ivy Light and her BFF dealing with the suspense of an angry spirit coming for revenge. Over the hills and through the woods...

At the end of the seventy-two hours, I turned in my manuscript, as the contest rules suggest you do, but I never received my certificate of completion. (Not to worry. I don't need a trophy to prove to myself what I accomplished.) Instead, I waited a few months for the story to fade in my brain, then revisited the manuscript in the spring of 2024. I edited the insanity and added scenes to blend a coherent storyline.

I reached out to my author friend J. Patrick Lemarr to connect me with his editor of suspense stories, Dani J. Caile, to see if he'd be available for editing help. Luckily, he was. He recognized I'd given a lack-of-prepositions colloquialism to every single character in the book. Along with correcting some other issues, he helped make *Silver Bells* presentable.

Next up, I reached out to horror writer Steven Shrewsbury to see if he'd have time to read the story and offer a foreword. His kind words are included now. My thanks to these three gentlemen!

The marathon was nearing its end. The finish line was in sight. All I needed now was a way to warn readers *Silver Bells* is not the light, satirical romp my Christmas stories are known for. This story contains strategically placed violence amid the Christmas tunes and cookies; there's blood on the snow drifts.

One way to offer such a warning is to release the book ahead of Halloween. Timing is everything. Another way is to state up front, in an introduction, this is a 42,000-word, suspenseful horror novella intended to give you shivers when you hear a bell toll.

Dive in.

Let's join Ivy Light at her best friend's home in Reindeer Creek for the holidays. We're all invited to enjoy the warmth and hospitality. Just be careful of the strange gray fog that swirls through with an uneasy spirit in its wake.

Have a Merry Christmas and a Happy New Year!
Sandy Lender

"Sacred places are the foundation of all other beliefs and practices because they represent the presence of the sacred in our lives." —Vine Deloria Jr.

"You shall call His name Jesus, for He will save His people from their sins." (Matthew 1:21)

Prologue

exie Stovall couldn't hear her younger sister over the roar of flames any longer. Her mother's incoherent wailing and the house's groaning drowned out Lizzy's shrill voice, shrieking at her cell phone on the back lawn: "Fifty-one Chestnut Parkway. It's fifty-one Chestnut Parkway."

Lexie pulled at her mother's arm, unsure what she shouted at the woman other than, "Come on!" Her own voice had become raspy with the heat and smoke surrounding her.

Pouring over her.

Infiltrating her.

"Get out of the house," Leland Stovall shouted from somewhere behind a wall of rising flames. From somewhere in the direction of the hall that led to the garage door, which, for some reason, he slammed shut.

Lexie's brain whirled with the stupidity surrounding her. What adult leaves the Christmas tree lights switched on all night? What mother pauses to pick out her favorite China figurines to save from the fire? What father drives his cars out of the garage when the structure is collapsing?

They've lost their minds.

"Come on!" Lexie screamed, nearly yanking her mother's arm out of its socket. She pulled her toward the open back door, toward the frigid snowy night, toward watching eyes from the tree line.

Chapter 1

A string of hollow sleigh bells thumped against the wooden door to announce Ivy Light entering the Under The Mistletoe boutique. As disappointing as their non-jingly *thunk* was, it assured the rest of the shop center stage. Cinnamon and nutmeg blasted Ivy before she crossed the threshold, stomping her tennis shoes on the forest green mat. It quickly collected snow and muck between rows of scratchy green brill that led to what looked like a grate below.

Efficient.

Karen Carpenter soothingly wished her "Merry Christmas" and "Happy New Year, too," from overhead, before a woman called, "Welcome to Under The Mistletoe." The voice forced joy from the depths of artificial trees, four-foot-tall painted nutcrackers, and freestanding shelves overflowing with garland and trimmings. The explosion of red and green consumerism inside the fragrant store hid the disembodied voice.

Holy cow. I'll never get out of here.

"What can I help you find?"

The voice's owner stepped from an avenue of shimmery golden fairy lights that appeared to lead toward the front counter. She wore a more

Halloween-inspired getup than anything befitting the winter wonderland atmosphere around her. Complete with wiry, gray hair under a black beret.

"Hi there. I'm looking for wine to take to a friend's house."

Despite the look of cosplaying an old crone, the shopkeeper tilted her head with a youthful manner. "I've got what you need. Back here."

Ivy followed the small sweeping gesture of the woman's black skirt as she swirled toward another trail through trees draped with monochrome bulbs. How many different shapes and sizes of red decorations did sweatshops in China export?

"I also have gorgeous wine glasses that make lovely gifts," the woman chatted as they meandered through the ornament forest. "I splurged and stocked some that have sterling silver stems."

"Wow. That sounds perfect for the clientele around here." Ivy struggled to think of something nicer to say. She hated shopping during calm and *non-busy* times of the year for a few reasons; chatting up commission-based workers was one. She never knew what the right blend of polite-yet-non-committal conversation would be. For example, right now, all she wanted was to buy a bottle of not too expensive wine to take to her best friend's house so she could hand it to Candy's husband as she walked in the door. This would solve two things—it would be a "thank you for inviting me" gift and a peace offering to Arthur.

"I said, are you looking for something dry or sweet? A dessert wine?"

"Oh, sorry. I was daydreaming. I haven't quite decided. Let me just stare at them a while."

The woman's smile turned from pleasantly sales-oriented to terse.

Great. I said the wrong thing.

"Of course. The merlots and cabernets are here in front of you." Her slick sleeve drew Ivy's eye along her arm and down a long black fingernail pointing toward a display of silver candlesticks, bells, picture frames, and baubles. "The chardonnays and other white wines are by the fine silver gifts."

As she spoke, the Carpenter tune overhead cut off mid-note and a pair of handbells began chiming the introduction to an old standard. Marilyn Maxwell's voice sang "Silver bells" over them as the shopkeeper continued. "Just beyond the silver gifts are some Grenache, our dessert wines, and some specialty wines."

Ivy tried to brighten her own smile, hoping to repair whatever offense she'd offered to this woman who looked somehow familiar. Maybe she'd offended so many of these poor shopkeepers that they all started to look similar when disappointed. "Thank you. I was told this shop had the best selection if I wanted an impressive gift. Thank you."

The woman's countenance didn't improve. "Of course," she repeated. "I'll be at the front if you realize you need help."

Ivy took a beat to consider the strange wording as the woman disappeared into the menagerie of holiday madness. *Wow. Get wine and get out.*

She turned on her heel and smacked into a man stepping into the aisle. Their impact suggested both were moving with purpose. It jarred the table of silver trinkets enough to knock over a clanging bell and an angel performing an already precarious pirouette.

"Oof."

"I'm so sorry," he said, catching her arm in a black glove.

"Holy crap. Sorry. Didn't mean to slam into…"

Now here was something interesting. Ivy had ploughed into a handsome fellow whose expression morphed from concerned to amused. *Wait. Is he wearing a top hat? What the Charles Dickens is going on in this store?*

His smile widened as if he understood why she lost her train of thought.

"Please tell me I didn't hurt you," he said. "I'd hate to get sued so close to Christmas."

"I look litigious?" she asked aloud. *Gawd, his eyes are actually lit up teasing me. How is that possible?* "Is this a Hallmark movie?"

"I beg your pardon?"

"Oh, God. I said that part out loud, didn't I? I'm pretty good at saying the wrong thing. Out loud. It's just that…" *Think fast.* "You're wearing a top hat in the year twenty twenty-four of our Lord."

He laughed lightly. "Nice one. You could've joined us in Carole Marrack's play. I've come from a small-town production of *The Christmas Candle* where I was an extra."

14

"Interesting. Isn't it a bit early in the evening for small-town productions to be over and done and the cast and crew to be out shopping?"

He released her arm to answer, and she wondered if the far-too-flimsy cardigan she'd worn for driving made her look frumpy. Of course, that thought probably motored through her brain because his hand had lingered with the sort of slow drag that suggested he memorized the contour of her wrist.

"One would think," he agreed. "But these small towns can't be inconvenienced for the arts." He lowered his voice conspiratorially. "The elite have balls and soirees to see to in the evenings."

She liked this banter with a stranger. He apparently had the same opinion of Reindeer Creek as she—it was overstuffed with new money and the socialites who enjoyed flaunting it. Ivy didn't have the kind of holdings that afforded a home in Reindeer Creek—be it new or old money.

"The elite parties are exactly why I stopped to buy fancy wine," she admitted. "I'm going to a friend's house for the holidays and wanted something impressive in my hand when I appear on the doorstep."

"Really? This will sound like a complete pickup line, but I'm here for the same reason."

A pickup line? If only. Look at yourself in the mirror, dude. Bring on all *the pickup lines.*

She missed the beginning of his explanation, but distinctly heard, "Even if I'm only there to guard the families, I thought I should have something impressive in my hand when I, how did you say it? Appear on the doorstep?"

"Wait. You're a guard? Like with the police?"

"Private security. But I've only worked for him for about six months."

Something about six months of private security tickled the back of Ivy's mind with familiarity.

"So, it's nice to be considered part of the family for the holidays. Even if it means posing as an extra in a play for the elite," he finished.

She could *feel* her lips exposing her teeth with a crazy grin on her face. "I'm kinda sorry I missed it now, but I had a couple of errands to run before I got into town."

Recognizing her complete discomfort and need to busy her hands, she reached to set the angel to right on the table next to them. "Couldn't fit local theatre in my schedule today." Here was the part where she buried her emotions and pretended it didn't still hurt to stop by her parents' graves on the way to visit old friends.

"Pity," he said. "I bet I could've had you added to my guest list. You know, free ticket to the show and all that."

Recovering her friendly attitude, she met his smile again. "The extras in the show get free tickets for family and friends?"

He spread his hands, palms up in open surrender. "I'd give it a try. Put the kind stranger I nearly knocked over in Under The Mistletoe on the guest list for John Knightley and let her sit in the front—what?"

"Your name is John *Knightley*?"

His lips smoothly curved into a half smile as if he'd practiced the following conversation a hundred times over the years. "Yes, my lady."

"Like the character in the Jane Austen novel?"

"Oh, I like that you reference the novel and not the movie. But I don't claim to be half as good as the gentleman Miss Austen created."

"The hat and gloves work so much more at this point. I'm intrigued, but also on a timeline. I've gotta purchase wine and move on down the road, or my friend will wonder if I programmed the GPS wrong."

He nodded once, bowing his head in character. "Hopefully I'll see you at one of the balls or soirees instead. If you're in town for the duration?"

"The duration?"

"Of the holidays."

She grinned some more. "Yes. I'm staying with my friend for the duration."

"I hope you don't mind me saying, you look extremely familiar for someone who's come from out of town. When you smile, I could swear I've seen you look at me like this before."

"Was *that* supposed to sound like a complete pickup line?" she asked.

He's freaking blushing. Oh my God.

"Uh, no, I hadn't intended to sound—I wasn't trying to make a move in the too-dark wine section of a specialty shop. It's just that I could swear I recognize you from somewhere."

She shook her head slightly. "First time in Reindeer Creek proper. In fact, I'm using this stop to grab wine for my friend and to reprogram the GPS to make sure I can get to her house without getting lost."

It pleased her that he remained friendly, not creepy, while they picked out a dessert wine they both thought would make a good statement upon entering someone's home. It was not so pleasing that he left the boutique with a flirtatious tip of his hat and "Have a Merry Christmas, Miss," before leaving her with the odd and still-offended shopkeeper.

"Is that all you need?" the woman asked coolly.

"You know? I think I want to get this little dancing angel I saw back there for my friend. Give me just a second. Oh, and do you giftwrap?"

The woman snickered. "Sure. It'll only take a minute and you can be on your way."

18

Chapter 2

I vy hadn't grown up in Reindeer Creek. The neighborhood had sprung up out of a forest that all the high school kids had treated as fodder for urban legends back in the day. That meant driving through the town of fresh roads devoid of landmarks required her GPS. As any unmarried forty-something with a good sense of humor does, she'd uploaded a sultry male British voice for the device. It seemed less patronizing to have a sexy Hugh Grant order her to "turn right in a quarter of a mile onto Chestnut Parkway" than a synthesized computer chick.

She chose to ignore the fact Hugh would use the metric system instead of her device's American units. Instead, she focused on keeping her Ford F-150's tires on the slick road when her headlights swept across a snow-capped, unfinished mansion as she turned from Apple Parkway to Chestnut.

"All this tax money and y'all can't salt the roads?" she muttered, squinting into the flurries her headlights highlighted before her. "Or maybe put bulbs in the streetlamps."

The light flurries speckled in the conical beams of her headlights, mimicking ash at the edges of darkness. Despite a waxing moon offering at least partial illumination, the snowbanks alongside the fresh black ribbon created the illusion of driving into a tunnel. To see better, she turned down the radio, so Bing Crosby barely crooned about every Christmas card he wrote. She instinctively kept the truck at a crawl, fearing black ice under the dusting accumulating along this road empty of any other traffic. Her hands gripped the wheel as if a tighter hold would keep the vehicle centered between the snowlines.

"Kinda silly to think this is the scary part of the drive," she mumbled. "Nothing to ram into out here."

Yet she couldn't shake loose the knot in her stomach as she glanced in the rearview mirror, half expecting the asphalt to open into a chasm behind her.

As she returned her hyper focused gaze to the front, a hit of adrenaline shot through her bloodstream. Her pupils dilated to take in as much information as possible.

A black shadow caught her peripheral vision before it bounded in front of the truck, and she slammed the brake to the floorboard. Fishtailing to a stop, she watched the enormous blob of fur bounce once in the middle of the lane and arc to the snowbanks on the left of the road. It nearly sailed with a gray mist clinging to its body over an iron fence set back twenty feet from the road and blended into the dark.

"Crap," she exhaled.

Her heart pounded from the fight or flight response as she stared, wide-eyed, into the darkness after the animal she'd narrowly missed.

"Put your dogs on a leash, people," she spoke to the soft purr of Bing Crosby.

Of course, she wasn't convinced the blob that had jumped so easily across her path was a dog. Too big. Too furry. But too fast and graceful to be a bear. *Has to be someone's Great Pyrenees. Or even a Scottish Deerhound.*

The lot onto which the canine had run was cast in flickering shadow from the neighbor's decadent holiday display. Of course, the two properties measured at least two acres each with homes built dead center to maximize space between humans. This meant the house with the clear bulbs lining its ramparts and lampposts wasn't on top of the dark one; wasn't casting immediate light on the disappearing dog. It offered enough illumination to prove Ivy was on the right track. She stared at the empty ruins of a recently burned home.

Candy had told her of this tragedy "down the street" where a Christmas tree fire had razed a multi-million-dollar mansion. Thank God the family had escaped with their lives, but this? This looked awful.

She watched the ostentatious display of wealth and festivity next door, then looked back at the still-smoldering char. *Wait. Why's it still smoking? This should've been out before the fire department left days ago, right?* And the day's snowfall would have covered and snuffed out any pockets of heat. There should be no smoke here.

Maybe it's fog.

She registered the idea that the crematory-colored smoke resembled the shapes of people crouched over to dig through the broken remains—wafting languidly along the rubble searching through ash. Part of her mind understood miscreants would wait for the cover of dark to look for treasure in a family's misfortune and might have their big dog along for protection.

Another part of her mind refused to believe the shadows were anything more than the movement of the decorations next door.

As she resumed her drive, cautiously, she glanced to the enormous house in the neighboring lot with a hint of disappointment shifting to ennui. Were the neighbors oblivious to the suffering next door? Or had they already helped their fellow man, and now moved on with life because that's what you had to do as an adult? The way of the world.

Hugh's voice burst into the cab, sending her a few inches off the seat. "Slight left in a quarter of a mile."

"For the love of God," she muttered. *Gotta settle my system before I get to Candy's and she sees how freaked out I am.*

She glanced in the rearview mirror, noticing a sheen of sweat on her brow. Sighing heavily at her nervous state, she gripped the steering wheel and crunched along the snowy street toward the Harris address. As she rounded the bend in Chestnut Parkway, she realized Candy's house had to be the one with flashing lights of multiple colors making the near horizon dance in the dark.

She pulled past the open iron gate, her headlights sweeping over a snow-drifted lawn of light-filled mechanical reindeer and colorful, rotund snow people. She drove up beside a recently parked Lincoln

Navigator® SUV, resisting the urge to plough into a mound of highly piled snow adjacent it, and stopped her truck. *Geez. Arthur's making bank. That thing's a Black Label.*

For a moment, she sat motionless in the driver's seat, both gloved hands still gripping the steering wheel as if she continued to maneuver through rush hour traffic. In sleet.

"Wait. Is that a *car* next to the monstrosity of wealth?"

Her own Ford F-150 dwarfed the scootie little smart car of diminutive size coated by a layer of snow. The tiny thing looked like a toy next to the Lincoln.

She now thanked her lucky stars she'd resisted the childlike urge to cap her maddening drive through weather-crazed streets with an explosion of snow by ramming the mound. She'd have sent someone's cute little "vehicle" shattering into the mansion's garage doors—plural—with her playful parking.

She giggled at the concept and worked herself back in a serious state of mind. She was about to enter holiday-land for two weeks with her BFF's unfolding family drama. Ivy came to this shindig as the token therapist but without the necessary certification. The scene to come required bracing.

Or the whole bottle of wine peeking out of her laptop bag.

She stared at the lights on Candy's house with a sense of pending doom creeping up her spine. The reds, greens, blues, yellows, and whites chased one another in time to Manheim Steamroller's *God Rest Ye Merry Gentlemen*. Loud, fast, and chaotic.

Seizure-inducing.

As the good Samwise Gamgee would say, "There's nothing for it." Ivy had to get out of the car and traverse the tidily shoveled walkway winding among Frosty gnomes and statuesque reindeer to Candy's monolithic front door. In fact, the fleeting thought of retreat evaporated as the front door swept inward—its substantial, over-ornamented wreath swinging momentarily from the motion—to reveal golden light spilling from a home of welcoming warmth. Ivy couldn't pretend to have been waylaid by some contrived responsibility. She grabbed her laptop bag and stepped from her truck to the frigid night air.

Wind whipped across the plains of Kansas specifically to smack her in the face. How did the snowman gnomes withstand it? How did the thousands of strings of lights remain in place, blinking their holiday cheer, against the bitter onslaught? She slammed her door, bent her head against the rush of winter, and trudged toward her excited friend in the patch of gold light.

Pine and evergreen with a high note of cinnamon met her halfway across the property. The house interior would be pungent with Christmas.

Candy's solid form silhouetted in the doorway waved her forward as if fanning the flurries into the over-nutmegged home. "Come on in." The alto voice achieved soprano range over the bastardization of the holiday tune swirling around the neighborhood.

Inundated with so much cheer, Ivy couldn't help grinning from behind tendrils of her own dark hair whipping about. Candy grabbed her into a bear hug, asking, "Have you been sitting out there in your truck?"

"I've been talking my nervous system out of a seizure from your light display."

Candy reacted to the compliment. "Isn't it great? Mr. Klauss from across the street helped Arthur get it finished up last weekend or I think we'd be working on it 'til New Year's."

"Mmm. It's visible from space."

Candy laughed one of the joyful laughs that suggested she'd been nipping at spiked eggnog. "That was my goal."

She turned toward the staircase thirty feet behind her and shouted toward the vaulted ceiling, "Harry! Arthur! Come help Aunt Ivy with her bags!"

"Nothing's gonna freeze out there," Ivy said. "There's no rush."

"You should see the finishing touches in the guest room," Candy squeed, as she crushed the front door closed against the winter outside. "It looks like the old playroom we had at my mom's house."

Ivy's brain teleported her to a summer vacation for a second. She envisioned an abundance of pink hues and a pair of Barbie Dreamhouse mansions amid an explosion of doll furniture, clothes, accessories, and, of course, dolls. Just as quickly as the scene of chaotic girlhood flashed in her mind with its plastic elbows and pointy hands posed for maximum beauty, the scene swirled back to the present.

Ivy smiled at the woman before her. Neither of them would be crawling around a pink carpeted floor with dolls over the next two weeks. But Ivy understood Candy had tried to match each of her guest rooms in this new home to childhood memories because Arthur had been designing it when her parents passed away. Their second child had died when the house was being built. They'd completed it and moved in when their only son graduated high school and prepared to leave the nest.

This whole place signified therapy.

The guest room Ivy would be staying in for two weeks had been photographed, videotaped, facetimed, and otherwise described in such detail that Ivy felt as if she'd already stood in it—as a child and as an adult. It boasted two bay windows facing a pond out back, had a hardwood floor that matched exposed rafters in its ceiling and fancy wooden frames around dozens of photographs of all shapes and sizes of Candy's family and friends. Ivy was being offered the most sentimental room of the house.

And she knew it.

"I can't wait to see it decorated for Christmas," she said.

This answer pleased Candy greatly. The woman squeaked again. "I even set up one of the Barbie Dreamhomes with freakin' Christmas décor. You're gonna love it."

As a forty-eight-year-old woman with a gaggle of transcription work to see to while on vacation, Ivy was pretty sure the Barbie Dreamhome décor would be a minimal distraction, but she was happy to appease her friend. "I bet I will."

"I'm sorry about the apartment downstairs," Candy said, pulling Ivy further into the foyer.

"Please. I fully understand. Where is everybody? Are they all down there?"

"I think so," Candy said. "There's an entrance off the garage that leads down to the apartment so they can come and go as they need to and not have to feel like they're interrupting the holiday planning up here. Marna was stressing about having to walk through the hall up here all the time. As if that would've bothered me, right?"

Ivy nodded, although she didn't know which of the displaced neighbors Marna was. She could guess that would be the mother who worried about inconveniencing the kind and lovely Candace Harris who'd taken her in. It was Candy's nature to talk about people as if everyone knew everyone else.

Friendly.

Open.

Like family.

Ivy knew to pay close attention to keep up and did so as she clomped along the hardwood floor toward the open-air kitchen. As they passed the wide, bent staircase, Candy shouted toward the vaulted ceiling again, "Harry! Arthur! Come help Aunt Ivy with her bags!"

"Who's Harry? Is he one of the Stovalls?" Ivy asked. It seemed logical that the Stovalls, staying in the apartment downstairs, would have a son who might be upstairs with Arthur in the movie room

Candy had talked about in rapturous tones. It would be a good distraction from losing one's house to watch movies with new friends.

But Candy surprised her with the answer that referenced her son, "Michael."

She released Ivy's arm as they crossed into the kitchen heavily scented of cookies and sugar. A layer of flour coated the marble island in the center of the room where a large metal mixing bowl and set of rolling pins awaited Candy's return. "He went off to college and decided people needed to call him by his last name."

"But Harry? Not Harris?" Ivy asked.

Candy grimaced, pulling an apron from a high-top stool. "Apparently. It took me the past week to get used to it."

Ivy giggled as she placed her laptop bag on one of the high-top chairs near the island. "It sounds way too grown-up for our Mikey." *As does college.*

She pulled the wine bottle from the bag and handed it over.

"Oooo…wine. You get to come visit more. Hey, this is the exact same one John brought us."

"John?" Ivy's brain clicked—all the gears moved into place. *Oh, God, no.*

"Yeah, Mr. Knightley."

"I knew I recognized you," a sultry voice announced from the open archway behind her.

Chapter 3

A timer dinged behind Candy, so both women turned away from one another.

Ivy's stomach flopped with what she hoped was mere embarrassment and not some kind of excitement at seeing a man she'd met half an hour earlier. But here was proof. Arthur Harris had hired private security for himself six months ago. Here was the bodyguard—staying with the family for the holidays. Candy's neighbor who organized theatrical crap all the time must have roped the Harrises, and their bodyguard, into acting in the season's play.

How bizarre that she'd run into the guy on her way to the house. Unless that was part of his job. Had she been followed into town? Had this guy tailed her from her parents' graves in Riverside two hours away from this new and posh community? Did he know she came from the poor side of the tracks?

"I thought I'd figured it out while we were at the store," he continued, now stepping into the kitchen and moving toward the island. "You looked like one of Candy's friends from some of the pictures she has up around the house. She'd assured me I didn't have to look into your background when you were listed as a person coming to the house for Christmas, so I didn't place your name. But you're Ivy, right?"

"This is my friend Ivy," Candy confirmed over her shoulder, lifting a tray of cookies from the oven. "I told you, we've known each other since first grade. Our entire lives, basically. We even went to the same college."

"Aunt Ivy!" a young man called out.

John stepped to his right as Michael "Harry" Harris barreled past him and flung his arms around Ivy's neck.

"I haven't seen you for ages," he exaggerated.

"Oof, holy crap, you're taller," she said, enveloping the kid in a hug. "How did this happen?"

"Ah, ya know. Mom makes me eat all that vegetable stuff." He released her, stepping back as if realizing he wasn't the high school "kid" she'd seen last time they'd all been together. He was an older, mature, college freshman now. He needed to conduct himself with some decorum.

"None of the clothes I bought you for Christmas presents are gonna fit," she teased.

"'s'okay. I'll change 'em all in for something a person would want."

"Okay, you two. Be useful." Candy pointed an oven mit at her son. "You, help John bring in Aunt Ivy's things, but run downstairs and knock on Lexie's door first. See if she and Lizzy want to help decorate cookies."

The lad clucked his tongue. "Those teenage girls don't want to decorate cookies."

"You don't know that until you ask. Go. Knock. Then help bring in things."

While Harry whined something else at his mother, Ivy smiled at John. "You don't have to drag my suitcase in here. I got—"

"I'm happy to help. Plus, I think it's part of my job description."

Candy pointed at him next. "Yes, as is the cookie decorating. I have twelve dozen of these to make fancy for tomorrow night's concert. Those who help get to eat the mistakes."

She placed a paper plate of broken tree-shaped cookies on the island before them while she spoke, as if offering up the example of mistakes. Ivy couldn't help noticing even the paper plates were Christmas-themed; some poinsettia explosion happened beneath the cookie parts.

"Those who don't help get nothing, either tonight or tomorrow at the concert," Candy warned.

"Hallmark movie," John quipped, winking at Ivy. He held a broken cookie part up to her as if in a salute, and bit off a corner.

She could feel the heat rising to her face as she recalled her flirtatious words at the shop.

"If you give me your keys, I'll start bringing—"

"Really, you don't have to schlep my stuff in. Harry and I can get it."

"Harry's gonna help me," John assured her. "And you appear to have not brought a winter coat to Reindeer Creek. Candy, did you tell your friend that it's cold here this time of year?"

"She knows."

"My heavy coat's in the truck." Ivy held out her arms. "This is a sweater that's not so bulky for driving."

John nodded. "I get that. But there's no point in you freezing out there. Keys?"

He popped the remainder of the broken cookie in his mouth as he held out his other hand. Ivy wasn't sure she should argue the point. It *was* ridiculously cold outside. Having the guys bring in her stuff meant all she had to do was point where to set it and then unpack. Easy. She acquiesced and fished her key fob out of her jeans pocket.

"Thank you," she said.

"You're welcome. And this'll only take a minute. I know which room she put you in, so we'll set things inside the door if that's okay?"

"Sounds perfect."

Ivy turned back to the cookie operation to see her best friend smirking at the dough she manipulated on the counter.

"Well then," Candy said suggestively.

"No."

"I think yes. What's the story, mornin' glory?"

"No story," Ivy said. "We met at the boutique picking out wine to bring here."

"Mmm-hmm. And that's enough to have you turning every shade of red under the sun?"

"I'm embarrassed is all."

"I can see that. What I wanna know is why. What happened at the boutique that's got you looking at our bodyguard like he's a movie star?"

"I'm not looking at—Seriously. We bumped into each other is all. Bought wine. Left separately. It's all a silly coincidence."

"So, what's the Hallmark movie quip? What did he mean by that?"

"*Argh*. You're reading stuff into nothing. I merely made a comment about Hallmark movie sets at the store."

Candy's smirk had grown into a full toothy grin at this point, complete with crinkles around her eyes and nose. She stuck her tongue between her teeth and laughed. "I think I'm reading exactly what's there. How great is this? So far, this Christmas has been a total flop with Michael's professor, I mean Harry's professor having to join us because his whole family came down with the plague and then the Stovalls lost their whole house in that horrible fire and, of course, you know, Arthur's strange attitude lately. I think it's great to have a little romancy fun around here."

Ivy put her hand to her temple. While it was a shame to learn of one sad event after another swirling around her best friend's life, she didn't want her own love life to be the shining star on the highest bough. Rather than dash Candy's moment of optimism and joy, Ivy put on what she hoped was a pleasant smile, and said, "I'm not going to encourage that line of thought, but you go ahead and think what you like."

As she expected her to, Candy giggled like they were back in school.

"What's happening?" John asked from the doorway.

"Absolutely nothing," Ivy answered.

"Is this something that stays in the truck?" he asked, lifting an egg crate in his right hand.

"Oh, no, that's stuff I have to finish wrapping. Let me…" *This'll send Candy into a fit of rapture.* "Let me show you where to set things up there."

Candy giggled more as Ivy relieved him of the crate, which was far less weighty than the suitcase he would be lugging up the stairs and around the bend.

"I've not been up to the room yet, so you'll have to guide me," she said.

"It's the first one off the landing up here," he said. "Wait 'til you see how she's decorated it. She's gone all out to make everything beautiful."

Ivy liked that. She liked the way he spoke kindly of her best friend's efforts. And because she never knew what to say, she said nothing about it as she followed him up the wide, curving stairs to a landing, which, on her left, afforded a view out an enormous window onto a winter scene from a blockbuster movie scene. The same moon that had teased her vision along unfamiliar roads now cast a blue glow and lacy tree branch shadows across the dips and swells of Candy's snow-covered backyard. When she looked to her right, she could see the entire great room with its brushed brass chandelier hanging above a blond hardwood floor and sparse, tasteful, expensive furniture set up to encourage small conversations.

The Harrises had a picturesque home.

As John opened the guest room door for her, she took in the wintergreen and mahogany mix that would be home for the next two weeks. As John had implied, Candy had decorated the room to be a magical winter wonderland. Ivy carried the egg crate into the homey space and set it on a trunk at the end of the queen size bed.

"You can put that suitcase anywhere. But there's a smaller one out there that'll go in the bathroom."

She looked to an open door next to a fireplace. From her vantage point, she could see signs of a clawfoot bathtub beyond the door.

"Here. Let me set this where you can unpack." He turned the suitcase on its side on the trunk next to the crate. "You didn't bring much stuff for a two-week vacation over a holiday."

"I figured Candy and I would be out shopping and doing girly stuff. I'll probably be talked into buying enough crap to fill another suitcase for driving home."

He smiled at that. "Sounds about right. I'd like to discourage too many excursions without the whole family if possible. I sent my backup home to be with his family for the holiday so I'm doing this security stuff solo. If I can keep everyone together, I can keep track of them more easily."

"You have trouble tracking Arthur?"

He puzzled at that.

"I don't mean to disparage your boss or put you in a bad spot," she said. "But Arthur's had some problems with fidelity in the past and Candy thought he was done with that. All grown up, right? But something's got her worried again, so I'm here to make sure she has all the support she needs if she has difficult conversations this month."

"Oh, wow. I didn't know that was even on the radar. Arthur's never stepped out on Candy while I've been on the job."

"That's good to hear." *I wonder if protecting Arthur's reputation is part of his job description.*

"He hired me to protect the *whole* family. That means I'm looking out for Candace Harris and her livelihood. I've got a man who keeps track of Michael, well, Harry, as he likes to be called the past four months, at the university. And, honestly, that's a more difficult cat to keep track of than Arthur and Candy combined."

She closed her eyes. "I don't want to think about Mikey being a player, thank you very much."

They could barely hear Candy yelling at the lad from the kitchen, "Harry, shut the front door!"

John chuckled. "I wouldn't classify him as a player. You can keep your good opinion of him. He's more into hanging out with these guys who play D and D instead of going to class. Alvin's had to intervene a couple times to keep him on the right track, but he's not womanizing up there at school."

"And Alvin's your hired help?"

John's eyes practically twinkled when he smiled at that. "Yes. Hired help."

"Well, bless his heart. My Mikey's just a harmless nerd." *Thank goodness.* "Good. I know I sound a little old-fashioned expecting an eighteen-year-old boy to stay out of 'girl trouble,' but I know Candy raised him to be respectful and smart. She and I grew up in a way that we took pride in who we are. I didn't quite act the part when we met earlier. Was it half an hour ago?"

A puzzled expression furrowed his brow, so she hurried to explain.

"I mean, I'm sorry I was all flirty and stupid at the shop earlier. It's not my *modus operandi* to chat up guys and act like I'm on the prowl. The clerk at the store was just a little weird and I was thinking I'd hurry up, get a gift for the house, and get out of there when I turned and barreled into you. So, I'm sorry for all of it and can we kinda forget my behavior?"

John was frowning through most of her speech and nodded absently. "We can do that. Start over? Reintroduce? But, you should know, I didn't find anything about you flirty and certainly not stupid. I'm not sure you need to go beating yourself up over some kind of behavior after I nearly ran you into a table of knick-knacks and then dropped a couple of really bad pickup lines."

She stared at him for a second. *So, those were pickup lines? Was he flirting with me then? Or now. All the Whos down in Whoville are confused.*

He smiled and held out his right hand. "Hi. I'm John Knightley."

I'm staring at him like I'm addled in the head.

She extended her hand to grip his as if they were meeting in a boardroom in downtown Kansas City. "Hi. I'm Ivy Light. Wait…did you say Knightley?"

Aw, yeah. There's that side smile.

"Yes, my lady."

Before she could respond, a girl's scream echoed up the stairs. His hand released hers and moved to the empty space at his hip as he turned for the door.

Because she'd followed the motion of his hand, she didn't see anything change in his eyes. She didn't see a cooled expression or firm set to his jaw. She didn't catch the twitch of frustration in his upper lip when his hand met with no weapon at his side.

Chapter 4

John Knightley rounded the bend in the staircase and slid down the banister the rest of the way in a quick, controlled descent into a frigid cold scene. The girl Lexie, whom Arthur and Candy had taken in, stood in her Goodwill flannel pajamas with nothing on her feet to protect them from the cold-and-getting-colder hardwood floor, and that lack of protection was becoming a point of concern. The teenager continued to shriek as she hopped from one foot to the other—in front of an enormous black wolf.

He couldn't see how the thing fit through the front door.

Candy had come to the archway near the base of the stairs and stood in shock, unable to assist the girl or move herself out of danger.

As he landed both feet on the floor, the uncomfortable jar of landing on breaking ice rocked the ligaments around his knees. But he wasn't stopping to assess the condition of his legs, the floor, or the merry synthesizer spewing a nineties version of "Jingle Bell Rock" through the front door.

He spied the cookie scribe tool in Candy's right fist, held near her shoulder in a fight, flight, or freeze response, and made a calculated sweep toward her on his way to danger. He grabbed the scribe from her, met her wide-eyed gaze, said "call nine-one-one from the kitchen" in his authoritative voice that typically brooked immediate action, and strode toward the wolf-like creature baring its teeth at the screaming teenager.

He wished Lexie could move behind the couch, give the creature a barrier to get around, but she appeared to have no capacity for self-preservation at the moment.

Harry had rejoined the melee with the business end of a solar powered stake from the yard. It looked like a much better weapon than the skinny pick used to manipulate icing.

"Distract it back to the doorway," he barked at Harry over Lexie's incessant scream-sobbing.

"What the hell's going on down there?" Arthur Harris yelled from the landing above.

"Oh my God. That's the dog I nearly hit on the way here," Ivy said.

Everyone's distracting everything but the wolf. It seemed laser focused on Lexie, never taking its eyes from the dancing-hopping girl.

Harry whistled as if calling a friendly beagle back from a romp in the park. "Here big fella. Look at me."

"What's wrong with you?" his father shouted from upstairs.

"Yes, I need police and help with a huge, wild animal that's in our house," Ivy's voice spoke clearly and confidently. "I'm at the residence of Arthur and Candace Harris at two fifty-seven Chestnut Parkway. This wild animal is *in* the house threatening a child right now."

Good girl.

For a breath, the noise stopped. As if the entire house inhaled John's step toward the creature's flank, the music outside paused, Lexie stopped screaming and sobbing, the wolf stopped snarling and growling, Harry stopped whistling, and Arthur stopped barking orders at his son. They were all frozen in the same snow globe second between the intro tinkle-bell chime and Mariah Carey's low "Eyeyeyeyeyeye" as John put his black tactical boot to the floor.

And the floorboard split with the gunshot of ice cracking apart on Big Hill Lake.

The wolf leapt for Lexie.

Tossing the scribe tool to his left hand, John lowered the weapon into an arc that matched his speed jumping to intercept the beast. As Lexie released a blood-curdling scream into Mariah's claim of non-consumerism, Harry dove for the animal. He caught its back leg mid-air, yanking backward and plunging the stake into its lower spine.

John wrapped his right arm over its neck. His left arm brought the weapon up, piercing the throat with the metal tip as he tackled the wolf from the front end, effectively knocking it off course and to the splitting floor. More gunshot ice-cracking rang through the house with the wolf's death howls, sending Lexie into fits of screaming while holding her ears.

The girl still couldn't run but danced in place frantically at the mass of fur, confusion, and coagulating blood at her feet.

Chapter 5

At the emergency room, Ivy paced back and forth in front of the mildew-blue curtain, listening to the social worker interrogating Lexie. She folded her arms across her upper abdomen as if protecting internal organs on Lexie's behalf. If she peeked behind the curtain, she'd no doubt see the teen hunched over to protect her vulnerable belly from the predatory woman firing questions at her.

"It's okay to tell the truth," the patronizing voice intoned. "I'm on your side. If someone burned your feet, we'll arrest them and bring them up on charges."

Despite the beeps and dings from machines and phones all around the bustling hospital space, Ivy clearly heard Lexie's response. "Look, I keep telling you. No. One. Burned. My. Feet. The floor was freezing because the front door was wide open. I don't get how that equals blisters, but it hurt like hell, and I couldn't run away because I was scared to death of the huge flipping *wolf* growling at me like it wanted to eat me for dinner. Okay?"

Ivy smiled to herself. Teenage angst was obnoxious when you were on the receiving end of it, but she had mounting respect for Lexie handling the constant barrage of leading questions from the social services woman who seemed to believe it was necessary to whisk Lexie to a group home for the holidays.

After a few minutes of quiet from the other side of the curtain, which Ivy assumed was for the worker to type into her Tablet, the calm voice of authority asked, "And where were your parents when the neighbor's dog attacked you?"

Ivy's right hand squeezed her left bicep almost painfully through the frumpy cardigan she had yet to remove since driving into town. Her own frustration was building to the point she'd soon be sprinting back and forth instead of pacing.

"Oh my God. You effing moron. It was a wild wolf that got into the house. A wolf. Did you type that into your little report there? It was a wolf. A wolf. A WOLF."

"Okay. Let's settle down. You seem too upset over this event. Maybe the nurse can bring you a sedative."

That's enough. No one's drugging this poor kid on my watch.

Ivy stepped behind the curtain. "Hi. I'm acting as guardian now. Please leave."

The neat and tidy social worker blinked from behind round-rimmed glasses. The pause lengthened while the three stared at one another. Finally, the authority figure asked, "What?"

"I said, I'm acting as this child's guardian, and you've been interviewing her without an adult present. Is that legal?"

"This isn't a police investigation," the woman snarled.

"It sounds like one. I invite you to leave now."

"I'll need your name and affiliation with—"

"Get out before I call security," Ivy said calmly.

Lexie blew a bubble with her gum. When it popped, the woman jumped. "Fine. I'll include in my report that a stranger was allowed guardianship over the minor."

"You do that. On your way out." Ivy compressed her lips to keep from saying anything further as the woman gathered her backpack and tools.

She crammed a small cloth doll into the satchel and shoved the Tablet into a front pocket. With a stylish wool peacoat over one arm, she offered a single scowl to Ivy before leaving the space. The fierce scrunch of metal shower curtain hooks rolling along the track above announced the "mood" of her departure.

Ivy waited for the woman's footsteps to fade into the confusion of the emergency room chaos before pulling the curtain closed with a calmer metallic swoosh. Then she dropped into the pea-green abandoned chair and looked at Lexie perched on the edge of the bed. "You gonna be okay?"

Lexie nodded. "That was bad-ass. I don't think I've even seen Mrs. Harris go nuclear on anyone like that. I mean, you were calm about it. Scary calm. That woman probably crapped her yoga pants."

Ivy laughed softly. "Thanks for the vote of confidence, but I probably got us both in trouble. She'll have half the hospital administration down here…"

Rather than dwell on the implications of a government-appointed shill telling hospital officials that she'd overstepped her bounds with an unrelated minor, she focused on helping the poor girl relax from her ordeal. "Well. We got her out of here before she gathered nurses around to administer sedatives and trick you into saying whatever crap she was after.

"Please don't get a bad opinion of social workers based off this one weirdo, all right? She had some opinion of what happened to you and figured she had to convince you to say it. I've got a couple friends who help kids who've been through trauma, and they do a very good job of it. They're not closed off and deaf like that woman was."

Lexie nodded at this. "Okay."

Ivy pointed at her feet. "Are you in pain?"

"Naw." She shrugged one shoulder indifferently. "They put some kind of numbing cream on the blisters before they bandaged me up. Took away the pain of another disappointing Friday night."

Ivy recognized the sardonic humor as a mask. "That's good. Do you think you'll *want* a sleeping pill or something to help calm your nerves? Do you want me to advocate for that?"

Lexie frowned. "I'm calm."

Ivy shook her head slightly. "I don't know why. I still have adrenaline coursing through me and I'm not the one who stared down a wild animal in a neighbor's house a week after losing my home."

Lexie gasped. "Wow. Harsh."

Ivy smiled sadly. "It's what that worker should've been asking you about. But not all workers for the state take their training seriously. Some come into their jobs thinking they already know how to help, whether that's true or not."

"And you know how to help."

Ivy laughed at herself. "Hardly. But I've picked up enough to be dangerous. I correct AI transcriptions for a bunch of doctors."

Lexie snorted a laugh. "Honest, at least."

"Yes, honest. And I'm being serious. Maybe I'm talking to you like you're a lot older than seventeen. But I want to make sure you're okay in there." She pointed to her own temple to indicate she was talking about Lexie's brain.

"Sixteen," Lexie said. "And there aren't a lot of grown-ups who would bother talking to me like I'm more than a first-grader these days. Everyone's been so flipping *careful* since the fire. Like they're gonna say the wrong thing to me and I'm gonna flip out."

Ivy nodded. "Full disclosure. I'm pretty good at saying the wrong thing all the time. So, if I do that here, I'm not doing it on purpose. I just can't help it."

Lexie chewed her gum, thinking on that.

"Example. I stopped at this boutique on my way to Candy's house this evening. Under The Mistletoe. Wanted to buy a bottle of wine, right? I said something that pissed off the shopkeeper and she turned from friendly and perky to weird and kinda threatening. Made me feel like I needed to make my purchase and get outta there in a hurry."

Lexie nodded at this, chewing her gum more quickly. "I've been in there. I bought my mom's Christmas present in there and, yeah, the shopkeeper was hella weird. She really wanted me to buy this silver ball ornament thing, but I couldn't afford it. I got this silver bells statue thing instead because it was only like forty bucks and that's what I'd saved from my allowance. It was like I'd ruined her commission goal for the month or something the way she treated me after I picked what *I* wanted."

They paused for a moment, Ivy recognizing the girl was about to reveal something important.

Lexie's gum-chewing slowed, and volume lowered. "Now even that's gone 'coz of the fire."

Ivy gave the statement a moment to live and breathe between them before saying, quietly, "Pretty presents can be replaced. Whether that's in time for this year, in time for a birthday next year, in time for a holiday three years from now, whatever you guys end up needing. I'm betting your mom's more thankful to have you and your sister alive and safe than all the trinkets and presents combined from your house."

Lexie sniffled back emotion and nodded without meeting Ivy's eyes. "People keep saying that."

"It's one of those truisms in life."

"Maybe," Lexie said. She took a moment before leveling Ivy with her dark eyes. "But no one saw my mom scraping the trinkets off her curio cabinet into a pillowcase when I was trying to get her out of a burning house. Not even Lizzy saw it 'coz I'd pushed her out back with her cell phone to call for help."

Oh my God. How do I respond to that?

Ivy swallowed the surprise rising in her throat. "She was in shock?"

Lexie shrugged one shoulder and blew a bubble with her gum.

"I've heard of people doing crazy things when in shock," Ivy offered. "When faced with extreme danger. Some people run in the opposite direction of the problem." She could tell Lexie wasn't buying the excuse. "Some people dive in with a kitchen utensil."

Lexie snorted at this.

"Some people stand around calling the police for help." Ivy pointed at herself. "Some people stare down the danger but are unable to run from it."

Lexie nodded, as if she understood this and might believe it someday.

"And some people probably freak out and see their future going up in flames. I have no idea what I'd do if everything I'd worked for was burning down around me," Ivy finished.

"Would you drive each one of your cars out of the garage and out of danger while your kid tried to get your wife out of the house?"

Wow. The whole family needs therapy to work through this tragedy.

She wanted to ask why they didn't have a fire extinguisher in the house. If Mr. and Mrs. Stovall had had enough time to throw valuables in pillowcases and drive cars out of the garage, the fire that had originated in the living room must have been containable, controllable, and smotherable. Shouldn't they have been able to stop it from engulfing their entire home?

Rather than pass judgment on Lexie's parents right there in front of her, Ivy said, "There are these self-help questionnaire things that ask you to prioritize what's important in your life by asking, if your house was on fire, what's the one thing you'd grab as you ran out the front door. It's easy to sit back in the safety of a therapist's office and decide which of your material possessions is the most important. But in the moment? If I was faced with that trauma? I have no idea how I'd react."

"I bet you wouldn't choose stupid figurines off a shelf."

Ivy smiled. "I already know what you'd choose."

Lexie offered her a quizzical look.

"Your mom and sister."

Lexie appeared to be thinking on that when they both stiffened at the approach of determined footsteps stopping at the curtain. "Lexie Stovall?"

Recognizing John's voice, they both relaxed.

"Yeah," Lexie answered.

He stepped behind the curtain waving a cell phone at her. "Your parents are on their way."

"Thank God," Ivy breathed.

"Yes, I overheard a woman at the nurse's station complaining about 'the Lettie Harris dog-attack case' and figured you'd be happy to get out of here sooner rather than later."

"The woman doesn't even have her name right?" Ivy asked.

He shook his head. "I'm about to think that's for the best. A red-tape nightmare might keep problems from compounding. You two look like you've been harassed."

"At least," Lexie muttered.

"I also brought socks and shoes from the house." He placed a knapsack on the bed beside Lexie. "But it looks like they bandaged your feet up too much to slide into your shoes."

"Yeah. I'm Frankenstein now. They're even giving me crutches so I can walk without putting weight on my blisters. How sexy will I look at the Marrack's party next week?"

John smiled at her and easily skirted the inappropriate question from a sixteen-year-old. "No one's looking at feet at a fancy Christmas party."

"Maybe no one *your* age," Lexie scoffed.

He turned to Ivy. "Candy's almost done giving her statement to the officers. Lexie's folks will be here any minute. Is there anything you need?"

"No, thank you, we're good. Do you need to get back to them?"

"I do. Who'd have thought guarding the family from a union boss hit would include protecting against wild animals straying into the house?"

"We should chat about the wild animal," Ivy said.

He nodded once. "I heard you on the stairs. About nearly hitting a dog on the way to the house. Let's talk about that when you get back."

Neither of them needed to point out the frazzled nerves of the young lady seated beside them to keep the details of the pending conversation to a minimum. It was as if they already knew how to talk to each other in code to keep Lexie settled and safe.

The teen snorted. "You two an item?"

Ivy put her hand to her temple, but not before she saw the sexy half-smile play across John's lips. "Now what makes you ask that?"

Lexie laughed at him. "That's a yes for sure."

"We just met this evening," he supplied. "I think we need at least another twenty-four hours before we can be considered an item."

Lexie laughed at him again.

Ivy avoided meeting his eye.

Chapter 6

The return trip to the house found Ivy struggling to stay alert. She rode back with John and Candy, listening to their conversation in the front seat while she drifted out of consciousness. At least, she attributed the vision of a large and lumbering wolflike creature keeping pace with the Stovalls' vehicle ahead of them to her dream state.

As Candy asked something about Ivy's availability to help teenagers shop for Christmas dresses, Ivy shook off the grogginess and met John's eye in the rearview mirror. If the creature were real, he surely would've seen it loping just past the shoulder in the dark. But he'd killed the predator earlier this evening; emergency personnel were clearing it from the house when they took Lexie to the E.R.; and now they returned to a house without any outward sign of danger.

She should have been able to relax.

Upon their return, Lexie's parents shuttled their eldest directly to the basement apartment and to bed. Ivy walked into the house to find Harry and Lizzy had placed a few sheets of plywood from the garage atop the splintered areas of the floor. It made a wonky walking surface, but covered the more dangerous places that could have tripped a person.

"There was a spot over here I think could have sent someone's foot through the basement ceiling," Harry said with a downward Ninja punch of his hand for effect.

Ivy shuddered.

John grimaced. "Thank you for covering things."

As if Harry understood all the bodyguard referenced, Harry offered a manly chin jut. "No problem."

"And where's your father?"

"I'm up here waiting for the family's protection to return to the house," Arthur announced from the landing above. "I watched over things while you were away," he explained, as if he were the alpha. "Now I need to run out and get some drop cloths and duct tape to cover the areas we didn't have plywood for."

Ivy watched John already shaking his head in disapproval of this plan.

"Shouldn't take me more than an hour to get to Dollar General and back."

Candy startled at this. "An hour?"

Ivy's problem with Arthur's plan was the destination, not the timing. "Wait. You have to go buy construction supplies? Don't you have—"

Arthur already descended the stairs as he snapped at her, "No, Ivy, I don't keep copious amounts of duct tape in my house. I'm not the mafia boss I've hired a bodyguard to protect myself from."

Ever the peacemaker, Candy stepped into Ivy's part of the conversation. "Ivy's merely asking why your company doesn't already have these things so you don't have to be inconvenienced by going out to get them at midnight."

"Let me run out to get drop cloths and tape," John interrupted. "You all lock yourselves in—"

"No," Arthur snapped. He marched across the expansive room toward the garage at this point. "No one's used a wolf attack to *lure* me out so they could kidnap me from a Dollar General at the edge of Reindeer Creek on a Friday night. Everyone, leave me alone."

Ivy offered a tight smile to Candy as she left the scene before its resolution, unwilling to listen to Arthur play the victim in a situation that, in fact, had never revolved around him. The conversation between John and Arthur played out in deep tones as Arthur offered some lame excuse for running to a store at midnight by himself instead of taking along the bodyguard he paid handsomely to protect him.

She ascended the stairs and turned the bend onto the landing, ignoring the asinine argument below. *He might be right that a random animal getting in his house isn't connected to a union boss threatening him, but why risk it? Why assume this* wasn't *a ploy to draw him out alone after dark? How crazy.*

She glanced down at the small group. Candy almost huddled in on herself, still in her winter coat with its faux-fur hood at the ready should she need to disappear under its comforting fluff. Harry stood with his Skechers hip-width apart as if squaring off against a foe, ready to defend his mother if Arthur should turn his current angst her direction.

Arthur completed the triangle, not quite slouching and not quite standing erect. If she believed him an alcoholic, she'd imagine him listing in the pose of the broken drunk. But Arthur was too egocentric to let any addiction have the upper hand. Something else weighed on him, pressing the man's shoulders inward and down—toward the plywood-patched floor.

The odd man out was John Knightley, who stood a hand taller than both Harry and Arthur. His navy-blue trench coat hung to the top of serviceable black boots that, like Harry, were set in defensive posture. And when she assessed this stance, she looked to John's face to see he glanced up at her. After a quick nod of acknowledgement to her, he returned his attention to his adversary. "If you're going out alone, take a weapon with you."

She moved past the moonlit window facing the tree line at the back of the Harris property and to her Holiday Barbie guestroom where she closed the door with a resolute click. Leaning her back against the solid wood, she closed her eyes and expelled a long, warm breath.

If this were a Hallmark movie, he'd let Arthur go to the store alone then come up here to tap on the door to check on me, right?

She half-smiled at her silly thought and rolled her head toward the first bay window to her left. Opening her eyes to take in the winter reflection, she wondered if this night were more suited for something streaming on Shudder. *Creepy Christmas shop with a familiar cashier leads to a crazy big wolf in the best friend's*

house. That's a recipe for Jason Statham to crash
through the garage with nunchucks and a Santa suit...

She laughed under her breath. "Or something."

Gazing at the bare branches across the backyard
only heightened her fatigue from it all. Time to
remove shoes and slide under the forest green
comforter to pass out. A shower and makeup removal
could happen at some point in the morning. In fact, as
she came down from the adrenaline high and agitation
that had swirled around her the past three hours, her
body overpowered her brain, making even shoe
removal difficult. She sat on the edge of the bed,
stared at her tennis shoes for a few seconds, and lost
track of time.

The scent of evergreen and snow wafted over and
through her, pressing her to the forest green pillows.
A rolling mist of gray, substantive fog clouded the
room, suffocating all sound save for a single, tolling
bell.

It smothered her.

From within the billowing gray, wolf eyes
blinked and winked while watching her sleep.

She couldn't move out from under their constant
gaze.

The mammals morphed and coalesced into bear-
like creatures, standing on hind legs to swipe at Lexie,
then a teen friend, then a gathering of men in fine
tuxedos. In the mist around her, another person ran
forward, eyes wide, mouth forming words she heard
as garbled, underwater screams. As Harry came into
focus, a wolf lunged for his neck, knocking him to the
ground, shredding him with tooth and claw.

Chapter 7

Saturday morning would see John speeding Mr. Arthur Harris out of the house for a meeting at his office downtown. John grumbled about it, saying all work was supposed to be remote the rest of the season. "I let Nick and Alvin go home for the holidays because we weren't going to be splitting up on a predictable basis," John said.

Arthur tossed back a morning scotch at the kitchen island, slammed the highball on the marble, and pocketed his cell phone before saying, "This isn't predictable. Isn't routine. No one's expecting me in the office 'cept my two supers who're gonna fix this ridiculous floor. We do this meeting and come back here with what we need to redo a floor that shoulda never split apart with a little cold air. Maybe you and I hit that indoor golf simulator place on the way back, eh? Work off some of the stress of last night."

Ivy had walked into the kitchen to grab coffee and lifted an eyebrow at John, questioning the concept of indoor golf. She clicked on the small radio next to the coffee maker and soft Christmas carols wafted into the tense room. The soothing tones were a blessing after the few hours of nightmarish sleep. *Trust Candy to keep simple beauty at hand.*

John shook his head. "That *sounds* unpredictable, but I'd rather keep you, Candy, and Harry in close proximity."

Ivy noted the snarl of disgust that curled Arthur's lip before he offered a fake smile to his bodyguard. "Sounds great. Let's go."

John grabbed a travel mug from the island and turned to Ivy. "Good morning. Do you gals have plans for the morning?"

"We wanted to take Lexie and Lizzy to some shops for new clothes. Shoes. And I think Candy added Christmas dresses to the list last night. If I understand right, the insurance company gave them an emergency check to live off of for a week or two and it basically afforded them nothing. They each have pajamas and a change of clothes from Goodwill. Teen girls need something more than that to heal a messed-up psyche, you know? They have three more days of school before the break, and all their peers are vultures and mean girls who'll crucify them for wearing the same things day after day."

He grimaced. "I guess I don't know a lot about teen girls' psyches, but I'll take your word for it. Can the shopping excursion wait until you have a bodyguard standing around? Is there anything you need to do here at the house where you can lock the doors?"

She grinned at him. "I have a thousand tasks for my needy doctor clients. But I think Candy's giving me a tour of the house. We didn't get to that with all the wolf and police excitement last night."

"It would be great if you could keep her at the house until I get back. Especially Harry." He looked toward the open doorway as if he could see the freshman still asleep upstairs.

"What's wrong?" she asked.

"I'm not sure why I thought I could send Nick and Alvin home for the holidays and handle the whole family on my own."

She resisted the urge to reach out and touch him. While it was natural to soothe a friend, she didn't really know this man. *It might be a bit forward to paw his arm.*

"I'm sure it was natural to want to give employees the holiday off," she said. "These three shouldn't be that difficult to corral. I'll make sure Candy and Harry stay home while Arthur's at work this morning."

"Thank you. And these two supervisors he's sending back to work on the floor?"

"What about them?" she asked.

"Don't let them in the house without us in attendance."

"In attendance?" she practically laughed. "Okay. Why don't you trust his workers?"

"Oh, I trust *his* workers. I've run background on all of them. I don't trust people who might show up *posing* as his workers."

"Mmm. Got it. Not letting random contractors in the house."

Chapter 8

After John had left with Arthur, Ivy realized she didn't have his mobile number and hadn't given him hers. If she needed to reach him in a hurry, she'd have to jump through some hoops. One of those hoops would be asking Candy for the man's number and enduring the teasing.

No one else was moving quickly in the Harris house that morning. Despite lack of sleep, Lexie wanted to follow Candy and Ivy on the tour of the house. Unfortunately, her crutches made navigating the stairs from the basement apartment to the first level difficult enough to park her in the kitchen with twelve dozen cookies and decorating tools instead. She startled at the cookie scribe.

Ivy saw her eyes fixed to the pointy tool.

"Is that…" Lexie asked, her voice trailing behind a veil of memory.

Ivy scooped the tool from the countertop, shaking her head slightly. "No. Candy has a few of these. But toothpicks work sufficiently for moving icing around on a cookie. I'll grab a box of those for you."

Lexie nodded, swallowing emotion as if everything were perfectly fine. "I don't know how to decorate cookies."

"Neither do I," Candy said, handing a small jar of toothpicks to Ivy. "But you're younger than me, thus more creative."

"Holy cow. How do you have so much icing?" Lexie asked, as if it had only occurred to her in that second that she peered at a mixing bowl heaped with red icing warming to room temperature.

"There are twelve dozen of these to cover," Candy explained.

"And this looks like enough to cover the house."

Candy pulled another mixing bowl from the industrial size fridge. "That's red. Here's the green."

"Oh my God. You guys."

Ivy picked up a shaker of multi-colored sprinkles. "This looks like a fabulous mess in the making. Will we get to help her after my tour?"

"There's plenty of work here," Lexie mumbled.

Candy set a stack of metal racks on the island, within arm's reach of the girl. "The icing will take a little time to cure before we can put the cookies back in the Tupperware for tonight, so place each one on the racks as you finish them."

"You've got a process for this," Lexie said.

"I did this for the Christmas concert last year and learned a couple tricks."

Ivy brought one of the aforementioned Tupperware containers from the long counter alongside the fridge to the island and opened it, releasing a mint and sugar blast of goodness. "Mmm."

"Oh, hang on," Candy said. "Those are the hint-of-mint ones. We ice those with white and use peppermint sprinkles so it's obvious."

64

Ivy and Lexie exchanged an amused look as Candy darted to the pantry.

"I think this is more complex than either of us realized," Ivy teased.

When Candy bebopped back to the center of the kitchen, she plopped a plastic can of vanilla icing on the counter and held up a Costco-size bag of peppermint candies next to her toothy grin. "See?"

"I sink those big candies in the icing?"

"No, we break them up into sprinkles," Candy said. Her excitement was unmistakable.

Lexie reached out with both hands to take the bag, frowning at this concept. "How?"

Ivy already had a plan in mind. *Please say it involves a wooden mallet. Please let me smash the crap out of that bag with a wooden mallet.*

"We use a meat tenderizer to crush the peppermints to bits," Candy announced.

Hell to the yes.

"Wouldn't candy canes be easier to break up?" Lexie asked.

"When was the last time you saw candy canes in a store?" Candy asked over her shoulder. She was already pulling a metal and a wooden meat tenderizer from a wide, shallow drawer of utensils near the oven. She held them in one hand while she selected a wooden rolling pin from the drawer as well.

Mm. One weapon for each of us. Excellent.

"I tried to find them last Christmas," Candy said. "No luck. Tried again the past couple weeks and gave up. But that bag right there is big enough to give us many cups of sprinkles. We just have to beat the crap out of it."

"Not a problem," Ivy said. *Hope I'm not salivating.*

Candy handed her the wooden mallet.

Hell. To. The. Yes.

"Do we unwrap each one of these?" Lexie asked dubiously, placing the bag in the center of the island between them.

"Not yet," Candy said. "The wrappers will contain the sprinkle dust. And the main bag will contain the mayhem we're about to create." She held the metal meat tenderizer out to Lexie like she was offering a high honor to the child. "Your weapon, my dear."

Lexie stared at the utensil for a second. Then she smiled. "This is gonna be lit, isn't it?"

Candy winked at her as the soft, low-end of a piano began "Silent Night" on the small radio behind her.

"Would you like to go first?"

Lexie looked to Ivy, as if for permission. "You guys are serious? We're gonna smash this with hammers?"

"This is therapy," Ivy said. "Go for it."

The young lady held the meat tenderizer near her cheek, her fingers wrapped around the handle so that her thumb crossed over her two center fingernails. As if in the far distance, Stevie Nicks' low, shaky voice began singing, "Siiiiilent niiiiiight."

With an unsure, unsteady arc, Lexie lowered her forearm, so the hammer struck the bag and bounced back. She watched its movement, then looked to Candy to make sure that was acceptable.

Candy pouted her lips into a contemplative, approving frown as she nodded. "Okay. Good first strike. Ivy?"

"Everybody back up," Ivy said. She zeroed in on one innocent peppermint at the corner of the bag and nailed it with the mallet, shattering it in one quick, lightning strike.

Lexie jumped but pretended to shake it off.

"Excellent form," Candy said. "My turn."

The rolling pin came down like a hammer on an anvil, splintering mint into the atmosphere of a voice suggesting "aawwll is caawwlm."

"Holy cow," Lexie said.

Candy winked at her. "Try again?"

Lexie changed her grip on the handle. "Yeah, let's do this again."

The young lady hit the bag with more force this time.

And then hit it again.

Yep. Therapy. Shepherd's quake at the sight. Ivy couldn't know what her best friend pictured when striking the bag of peppermints, but Ivy imagined wild wolves and negligent parents who distressed teenagers, cheating husbands who endangered best friends, unreliable clients who caused financial mayhem in her own life, holiday traffic, spooky shopkeepers, disturbing nightmares, and all manner of stress she couldn't put a name to.

Among the three of them banging, smashing, and crushing the bag now bouncing like a downed piñata,

Ivy figured they'd destroyed the chances of separating plastic from sprinkle. Sugary, minty freshness filled the air and bits of sharp candy stung her cheeks. But she didn't care.

Lexie had changed her grip on the meat tenderizer handle again and now held it with both hands, slamming the hammer repeatedly into the mints, crying as she hit a renegade piece that slipped the bonds of the ruptured bag. All three of them were laughing through tears at this point.

"What's going on in here?" Harry asked from the doorway. He obviously wasn't coming any closer.

Candy dabbed at her eyes with her fingers, laughing too hard to answer him. Ivy yanked a towel—inscribed with the message "coffee's a hug in a mug"—from the fridge doorhandle and offered it to Lexie. She tried to talk through her own tearful laughs, "Just blowing off steam. It's all good."

Lizzy tip-toed up behind Harry. "Are they okay?"

"I think they're having a group nervous breakdown," he suggested lowly. "We should steer clear."

"And that!" Candy announced. "Is how you make peppermint sprinkles for decorating a few dozen Christmas cookies." She accepted the wooden mallet from Ivy and carried it with the rolling pin to the sink. Both instruments were sticky with candy and plastic bits.

Amid the joyful chaos, no one noticed Lexie rest her minty weapon on her lap for safe keeping.

Chapter 9

During the tour of the house—which impressed Ivy greatly—the women talked in hushed tones about an idea Candy had for a different sort of tour. She wanted to explore the ruins of the Stovalls' burned house to see if there was anything she could salvage, clean, and present to the family as a keepsake for the future.

"Oh, sweetie, that sounds really lovely and all, but are you sure that's safe?"

Ivy was worried about more than John discovering them out of the house, separated from Harry and the girls. She honestly didn't know how structurally sound a burned house would be. Would they be physically safe trying to walk on a leveled building that had a basement under it?

But Candy was determined and her argument that the floor was made of a composite and rebar base— thus able to support the women even after the fire— won in the end. She produced a pair of canvas shopping bags and two pairs of work gloves for the adventure. "It's kinda cold to walk down there. Can we take your truck?"

Ivy thought that was the smartest part of the ill-devised plan. If anyone was out to harass Arthur's family, they hopefully wouldn't recognize Ivy's vehicle.

"Okay. Let's see what we can do. And you can fill me in on something." The idea of someone harassing the family put another question in her mind. *Who* was harassing the family? Candy had shared, about six months ago, that Arthur had hired private security to keep them safe, but she'd been a little fuzzy on what he was keeping them safe from.

Candy took a long approach to explaining it, and the women were helping each other over mounds of ash and burned wood by the time she got around to blaming a couple of local construction businesses that were in competition with Arthur's company. She explained that those businesses were locked in with a local union run by regional business mogul Mr. Dayton Manti. And there was the problem.

Arthur refused to join.

"There was a time in our history when unions helped get basic working conditions set straight for people, but that time is in the past," Candy said. "The unions now are just another arm of the government taking wages from their members and exerting control over the use of our tax money. If Arthur bends to their influence, he's got to play by rules that neither of us like. I'd rather he keep his soul intact."

Ivy chuckled. "Tell me how you really feel."

"I'm serious. He might be acting like a jackass in the marriage department these days, but he's never been unfaithful to his employees."

Strange defense. Does she really think he's a different person from one sphere to the next? That he's a better human in business than in family matters?

"He pays those guys—and gals—more than the going rate," Candy continued. "And takes better care of them than those companies where they're following employment law only to the letter. Where they're doing the bare minimum that they've been dictated to do. The state's got it set up so he can't even bid on a project over a certain dollar amount unless he's employing union workers and playing by union rules, which are less than what he's doing for the people he cares about. I don't see how that's legal."

Ivy frowned, trying to stay focused on the business sphere Candy was focusing on. Whispers on the wind threatened to distract her and sent a chill through the fluffy down coat she wore. "Me neither. How does the government get to pick and choose among the low-bid system all of a sudden?"

Candy bent to lift a glob of material out of the ash while she answered. "I think they get around it by keeping the contractors they don't like from bidding. It's very nineteen-thirties mafia-like to me." She shook the material vigorously to dislodge its crumpled, frozen folds and knock ash away.

"Government as mafia?" Ivy asked. "Sounds about right for the times we're living in. And makes me feel exposed out here without any cover. A government sniper could be hiding in the tree line to take us out."

Candy poked her tongue between her teeth and giggled, which, to be honest, wasn't the response Ivy expected. "Can you imagine? Arthur designed and built our dream home at the edge of this fancy new neighborhood so we could be along the protected land, right? We wanted to have the strip of forest giving way to prairie behind our property for as long as possible, thinking it would remain protected at least until the legislature got around to voting to hand it over to some greedy corporation. Now here you and I are talking about union assassins hiding out in that very strip of forest."

The two paused to look at the tree line. Naked, bony branches reached into the gray sky of winter.

"And Arthur's already having to fight to keep it protected."

"Already?" Ivy asked. "You guys only finished building a year ago."

"Yeah. He's got a meeting with the county commissioners this week or next. Sometime before Christmas. Imagine an architect with an entire construction workforce trying to convince county commissioners to *stop* people from taking a bill to the state to clear the way for progress."

Ivy looked to her friend's faraway gaze. *She's got too much worry for one person to take on.*

"But if the union wants it done, I don't think we'll be able to stop it," Candy said. "They have too much money. And we'll have a car wash behind our pretty pond."

Ivy couldn't help grinning at her. "A car wash?"

Candy grinned back. "First noisy business that came to mind."

"Oh, come on. You don't think a bowling alley would be more interesting?"

Candy started to laugh. "Gawd, I'm glad you came for Christmas this year."

"Me too, girlfriend. I'm sorry I wasn't here last year." She felt the weight of having failed her friend press her chest, shoulders, bones. "I'm sorry I didn't find a way to get here."

Candy waved a hand as if this were a trifle, but she couldn't find words.

Or her voice.

Or both.

Ivy spoke softly in the cold air, "I wish I'd found a way to come to your first Christmas after losing little Mindy."

Candy nodded, looking back to the leafless trees in the near distance. "You were here for me when she passed."

Ivy pressed her lips together, holding information inside. She'd never share what a financial hit she'd taken to leave her business at a critical moment to tend to Candy while the woman healed from a miscarriage. She'd do it again in a heartbeat if needed. But that financial hit was what prevented Ivy from making the trip a second time in a calendar year for a mere holiday. It was what prevented her from getting over to Kansas to see Mikey—now Harry— graduate from high school in May. She'd missed a huge milestone in her dearest friend's life this past year and that fact hurt her heart.

"I wish I'd been here consistently for you. A couple of long phone calls a month doesn't offer the same therapy as being here in person. Especially at the time of year when family's supposed to be together. The people in your circle seem to have forgotten the reason for the season. Talking about tearing down trees and forcing your husband into hiring a different workforce? These are not happy holiday topics."

"This might be." Candy deftly changed the subject by holding up the shirt she'd shaken out. Her chunky work glove fingers resembled clothespins along the top edges of it. "Does this look salvageable?"

Ivy reached over charred mess to accept the material. "Maybe." There was nothing remarkable about the girl's shirt Candy had found. It was obviously fire-resistant material. Blue and green colors blended into a swirl of pastel creamery behind soot and what looked like the edge of a greasy footprint at the hem. *I doubt we can clean this.*

"Let's take it to the dry cleaners and see if they can save it," Candy said.

Ivy smiled at her. "I love your heart."

"Right. Let's see what else we can find in this nightmare."

They dug carefully through the mess for another hour. Between the cold seeping into Ivy's bones and the increasing potential that John could return with Arthur and catch them at this dangerous task, she grew more anxious to stop.

"Do you think we should call it?" Ivy asked across a skeletal mound of burned furniture.

Candy moved gingerly toward the mess. "We probably should. The basement stairs are completely blocked, and I haven't found anything up here for the past half hour."

"I'm telling you, I could swear there were people out here last night. If there were treasures to rescue, they stole them."

"I hate that idea," Candy said. "What kind of cretins steal from a family who's already lost everything?"

"Cretins who have no Christmas cheer. What? You look concerned."

"Hang on." Candy knelt to smooth ash at the edge of the furniture pile. "Do you suppose the firefighters threw this furniture here? I mean, this looks like a strange mix, right? Bed frames, chair frames, table legs, lamp legs…"

Ivy agreed it was a strange mix to be lumped together but she didn't know anything about putting out fires. *Do firemen take time to chuck heavy objects in any particular direction for any particular reason?*

Given what Lexie had said at the hospital the night before, a shocked and motivated Marna Stovall could have thrown any number of heavy items clear of her path as she moved through the house.

"I don't know how they clear a house," Ivy said. "What'd you find?"

Candy held up an oxidized silver chunk of ornament to the hiss of ash crumbling away under one of the bed frames between them. With a puff of soot mushrooming upward, the pile collapsed in a startling clunk and clank of ruined metal and brackish icicles.

Ivy waved her gloved hand before her face and coughed against the fine detritus.

"Ugh. Mess," Candy said, stepping back from the collapse. She dropped the silver blob into the bag of what few treasures she'd recovered.

From the tree line, a wolf howled.

"Time to go," Ivy said.

Chapter 10

Candy convinced her to swing by the dry cleaners not far from the entrance to the posh subdivision so they could drop off the shirt and a strip of quilt they'd found. The owner clucked her tongue and shook her head sadly as she examined the two pieces.

"That's a sad, sad shame what happened to that family. Praise God no one was killed in the blaze. I guess that's why we're all supposed to turn those tree lights off at night before we go to bed. It was the tree lights, wasn't it? Didn't the fire marshal say it was the Christmas tree that set it all off?"

Ivy let the two locals discuss the tragedy while she looked out the front window. Gazing between the painted letters advertising holiday curtain, gown, and tapestry cleaning specials, she watched traffic sliding and honking through the badly designed parking lot.

People were descending into their Christmas shopping impatience with one another and the road rage on display in this small town of fancy cars proved it.

What a shame. Don't these people stop and chill for the season? Maybe beat up a bag of candy to alleviate some stress.

Candy's touch on her arm pulled her from her reverie. "She thinks she can clean the shirt so it's wearable again. She's gonna do some trimming and cleaning to get a scrap of the quilt to look nice again. Both will be ready on Thursday." She was tucking a slip of paper into her purse.

"That sounds amazing." She wanted to say Marna would be thrilled by the gesture, but after the conversation with Lexie in the E.R., she wasn't sure what Mrs. Stovall's reaction to fabric-as-heirloom would be. Instead, Ivy smiled for her friend and said, "We should get back to the house."

"I'd like to stop and get a shadow box—"

"When we're out shopping for clothes, you can stop all the places you like. I'm your driver extraordinaire this afternoon. Right now? Back to the house before any bodyguards discover I failed in the *one* assignment I was given today."

"One assignment? What was that?"

"To keep all of us at the house together."

Ivy not only failed to keep everyone at the house together, but she also failed to hide her failure. As she drove the truck into the driveway, her heart thudded against her ribs. She was caught.

John held the Black Label SUV's back door open for Arthur to climb out.

*****

The sheepish look about her amused John for a second. *I hope she doesn't think I'm gonna yell at her or something.*

78

"Did you ladies go shopping?" he asked, pointing at the two bags Candy carried.

"Dry cleaners," Candy supplied, but she was already distracted by one of her mechanical reindeer with a broken horn. "Oh, my goodness. I didn't even notice this when we left. I bet that stupid wolf-dog thing broke some of my lawn ornaments last night."

She handed the bags to Ivy so she could more easily fiddle with the deer and its strings of lights.

"We have workers on the way to the house right now," Arthur said. "They can fix any of these deer or gnomes or whatever if you need them to." He moved toward the front door; his service for the day was complete.

The figures lining the sidewalk looked like cheery snowmen to John, rather than gnomes. But what did he know about lawn décor? He'd never put a lot of thought into the concept.

"Aren't they coming to work on the floor?" Candy called after her husband. "Inside?"

"Yeah, but they can do whatever you need them to," Arthur called back. He was already entering the house, yelling over his shoulder. Again, his service for the day was complete. He was a king returning to his castle to relax, not deal with broken lawn ornaments.

"They don't talk *to* each other, do they?" John observed absently.

"Not like they used to," Ivy said, bringing a waft of peppermint and ash near to him. "Sorry about leaving. Candy wanted—"

"You don't have to apologize. I'm glad you went with her. She shouldn't be out alone if crazy people are threatening the family. Having a friend at her side makes her less of a target."

She smiled at that, and he liked the expression. It distracted him from the worry that he suspected she had soot on her tennis shoes—like Candy had on her boots.

"Do you—do you have peppermint flakes in your hair?"

She closed her eyes as if blocking out the strange question.

"I'm not trying to be judgmental," he hurried to say. "It just looks like candy flakes, and you have this yummy mint scent going on."

"Yes, yes, that's peppermint. We crushed peppermint for the cookie decorations before we left."

He couldn't decide if that was funny or amazing. Or both.

"Hey, guys, I think it's great that you're having a moment, but I'm about to freak out," Candy said.

They both looked at the woman who stood, about five or six paces away, facing them. The color had drained from her face and her breath fogged from her rapid breathing. She pointed to something behind them, on the other side of the snow-covered smart car.

Following the pointing finger, they both turned to see, on the far side of the driveway, a growing gray mist billowing around a wolf. The beast sat on its haunches, staring into Ivy.

"Oh my God," she said.

"Whoa. No fast movements," John said. "You two walk slowly and calmly to the house. Go inside. Call nine-one-one from inside. I'm right behind you."

"What are the chances a second—"

"You should be moving to the door," he said.

What puzzled him was the wolf's direct gaze. It continued to watch Ivy, but its eyes shifted, lowering as if watching her hands, watching the two bags she carried toward the house. *Why would a wild animal be interested in dry cleaning? Can it smell chemicals I can't?*

He'd learned his lesson the night before and wore his gun at his hip today. Although his heart currently pounded like a bass drum in his chest, he knew he could draw on this beast and take it down if it leapt for any of them. He'd rather not discharge a weapon in suburbia, but, when faced with a wild animal leaping for your throat…

When he heard the door open behind him and knew the women were safe, he began stepping backward toward the house as well.

As if this was what the animal wanted, it rose and turned in one fluid motion. It loped with the gray fog swirling and sticking to its coat toward the backyard.

Chapter 11

Ivy noticed Lexie shivered from time to time while she iced cookies and listened to John on his phone with the authorities. The poor girl probably had the same *unsettled* feeling Ivy did at learning a second wild creature stalked the house.

"Yes, I consider it your responsibility to handle it if there's a pack of wolves roaming a suburban neighborhood. Is that not what animal control is supposed to do? Control animals?"

Ivy smiled across the island at the two teen girls working to complete the cookie project. "Two wolves is not a pack," she told them quietly. "Especially when one of them is already dispatched."

"I'm not freaking out," Lexie assured her.

"I'm kinda freaking out a little," Lizzy said. "If he killed one of their pack, will the rest come here for vengeance?"

"This isn't a sci-fi movie," Lexie told her. She chewed her gum a little faster.

When John touched the "end call" button and set the phone on the counter behind him, he lifted both hands to his face and rubbed the stress from his temples.

"Mr. Harris does that before he drinks," Lizzy whispered.

Candy swept into the room then to assess cookie progress and confirmed they had enough for the church event that night. She relieved the girls of their task so they could get ready for a shopping excursion that afternoon.

With the teens excitedly rushing off to the basement—one hobbling on crutches in a most hurried and flurried manner—Candy set a plastic tackle box on the island and carefully moved the metal rack system with its last few drying cookies to another counter.

"What's this next project?" Ivy asked.

John walked over to sit at the island with them, watching Candy remove silver polish and rags from the box.

"I want to try to clean up that statue I found at the house."

"At the house?" John asked.

"Oh, yeah, I didn't mention…" Candy let that idea trail away.

He sighed. "Animal Control seems disinterested in wolves randomly walking among the humans in this neighborhood, so it might be a good idea not to visit burned out houses alone."

"Ivy was with me."

He glanced at Ivy, who avoided meeting his gaze by straightening a towel on the counter for Candy.

"That only comforts me when we're talking about discouraging Arthur's enemies from harassing you in public. I don't know the motives of wild wolves loping over from the protected prairie beyond the tree line. Let's avoid attracting them like a lone wildebeest separated from the herd."

"Are we being compared to wildebeests?" Candy mocked.

"The small, cute ones," he said.

"Hmm. I think you should be off guarding my husband somewhere else in the house."

He chuckled at her teasing tone. "In a minute. First, Ivy and I haven't had a chance to talk about this dog she saw last night."

"What dog?" Candy asked.

"Oh, yeah. A dog ran in front of my truck last night. When I was driving here from the Christmas shop. I was already on Chestnut Parkway, and this huge dog bound across the road." She looked to John. "I hit my brakes and missed the dog, but it ran to the Stovall property. It looked like there were people digging around in the ruins so I thought it might be theirs."

He nodded along. "But when you saw it in the house threatening Lexie, you recognized it?"

"Well, not it, so much. But I recognized the size of it. The thing was big and hairy. Very dark."

"Like the one out by the driveway a little while ago?" he asked.

She felt the weight of that idea press down on her. "Yes. Like that one."

John sighed. "We should probably keep anyone from going outdoors alone until we're sure Animal Control has taken care of the problem, or the thing has moved on." He looked at the oxidized ornament Candy worked with.

She'd unscrewed the cap from a polish container and poured a generous amount of chemical-smelling gel into a bowl of water. Without bothering to mix it, she dunked the ornament in the bowl, completely submerging it, and swirled it gently so as not to slosh the liquid over the edge. Ivy recapped the stinky polish container.

He frowned at the ornament. "How did that not melt in the fire? I'm assuming that's from the Stovall property?"

"Yeah. I found it at the edge of some furniture, kinda protected by a crisscross of metal stuff." She shrugged while she spoke. "It might've been protected from the main fire. Or maybe the main fire had burned out before it got to this. I don't know."

"Fire moves in strange ways," Ivy mumbled. Speaking more clearly, she said, "We found a few metal things. A picture frame. A lady's brooch. A couple utensils. They might not have any sentimental value, but we figured we'd clean them up and if the Stovalls want them…"

"That sounds very kind," John said.

"Candy's got this nature about her," Ivy said.

They watched Candy lift the ornament from the bowl and towel it off before dunking it in again. She swished it carefully while saying, "It might be a fool's errand, but it gives us all something to do while they fight with the insurance people. Isn't that where they are again this morning?"

John sighed into his answer, "Yes."

He's trying to keep track of all of us. Poor guy's gonna lose his mind at this rate. Right along with Lexie and Lizzy.

"It's a shame they have to deal with this at all," Ivy said sofly. "But the time of year is almost heartbreaking. They're at the age where they don't expect a visit from Santa, but there should still be that sense of expectation at Christmas. There should still be hopeful and peaceful memories being made." She paused while the three of them watched the silver drip inky water to the bowl beneath it as Candy lifted it carefully, gently. "There should still be moments of excitement and wonder for Christmas."

Candy lowered the ornament back in the staining water and smiled across the island at her. "I agree. And we'll do what we can to remind them what Christmas is about."

John nodded along with this sentiment until he frowned. "Wait a minute. The stuff in those two bags wasn't from the dry cleaners?"

Ivy puzzled over his question for a second. *Why does he think we had dry cleaning in shopping bags?*

"No. We dropped stuff *off* at the dry cleaners," Candy explained.

"You're saying the stuff in the bags was from the Stovall house," he said.

He looks really worried about that. Why's he worried about that?

"Can I see what else you gals found?"

"Sure. Bags are on the counter there," Candy nodded toward the pantry over her left shoulder as she lifted the ornament again. She toweled it again, scraping and scrubbing with her thumb through the terrycloth this time.

Ivy followed John's movement across the kitchen. Man, some guys looked deathly handsome in a pair of jeans with tactical boots. He looked like he could take down a wolf in the living room with an ice pick—or cookie scribe—or whatever utensil happened to be on hand.

"Excuse me," Candy whispered.

Ivy darted back to the present, locking her eyes to Candy's. "Hmm?"

The amusement on Candy's face promised a full teasing later. "I asked if you would open the cream polish for me since your hands are free."

Heat rose to Ivy's face as she reached into the tackle box for a tube of the requested silver polish. But something distracted her from her embarrassment. The ornament in Candy's hands took on familiarity.

"Hey. Silver bells," Ivy said.

"Yeah, I'm sure this is a Christmas ornament. It looks like it's broken, though. See how the flowing ribbon part across the top here overlaps? There's a stem in there. There's supposed to be a handle. At least, I think there's supposed to be a handle. That part must've broken off."

"Is it heavy?" Ivy asked.

"Not too much."

"It might be the gift Lexie was telling me about last night."

John walked back to the island with one of the bags, taking an interest in their conversation. He examined the ornament they discussed.

"She said she'd bought a silver bells statue for her mom at Under The Mistletoe. It cost her forty dollars. Doesn't that look like a forty-dollar-range gift?"

"If it's real silver?" John said. "All the way through? No. I'd expect that to be a lot more expensive than forty dollars. But if it's silver plated—maybe so."

"It's a pretty big coincidence to *not* be the gift Lexie bought, though, right?" Ivy asked.

"I'd think," Candy said. "Let me see if I can get it clean."

"Was it in this bag when you came back from the dry cleaners, then?"

Ivy and Candy both nodded the affirmative.

"Interesting. I could swear that wolf out there was more focused on these bags than on any of us. I even wondered if it was smelling dry-cleaning chemicals and if that was what had attracted it into the open. Into broad daylight. Now that you tell me the thing—or its pal—was at the ruins last night, I have to wonder if there's something they're hunting for."

"You have officially freaked me right out," Candy said.

"You've gotta be kidding," Ivy said. "Are you suggesting a pack of wolves is sentient enough to hunt for objects in a burned-out house and then, what? Follow those objects in shopping bags humans carry away from said burned-out house?"

John laughed lightly. "It does sound crazy when you phrase it like that."

Chapter 12

As hectic as it seemed on the surface, Ivy was grateful for the distraction of crowded stores and fussy fellow shoppers that afternoon. The predictability of it reminded her of re-watching old movies. You knew the ending—even if you knew it ended in death and destruction, you had the comfort of foresight.

Going to a clothing store where all she had to do was sit back and wait for a pair of teenagers to pick out jeans and tops was almost comforting. Waiting for Candy to select a shadow box and sprigs of mistletoe at a craft shop was peaceful, despite the gaggle of older ladies arguing over pics and ribbons.

They used the excursion away from the house to let the contractors fix the great room's split flooring under Arthur's supervision uninterrupted. It took Candy nearly an hour to find a housecleaning service who could come in to handle the dust that afternoon. She was determined to remove all signs of the frightening intruder—and its cleanup—by the time her guests returned to the house.

They only had one mishap at the mall when John nearly accosted a young man approaching their group. Young Ezekial Shah turned out to be Lexie's boyfriend, so no one had to be interrogated or reported to police.

"Why haven't I heard your name before now?" John asked the kid.

"I go by Zeke at school," he said, as if that explained why Lexie hadn't mentioned him.

"My mom doesn't know about him," Lexie said.

Lizzy whispered to Ivy, "He's listed as 'Eke' in her phone."

The situation didn't make a lot of sense to Ivy, but she figured she was out of touch with today's youth and their ways of hiding relationships from parents—parents and the neighbors' private security.

She whispered back to Lizzy, "Do you really think your mom doesn't know about a mystery boyfriend?"

Lizzy rolled her eyes as she returned to the rack of long-sleeve t-shirts she flipped through. "*Marna* has no clue what either of us does. She's got a glass ceiling to shatter."

When Lexie's feet began to hurt from the exertion against her blisters, they stopped for food and made their way back to the Harris house to rest before the Christmas concert that night.

Another comforting familiarity, Ivy told herself. She anticipated enjoying traditional hymns that would lull her into the tranquility of the season. As they did in childhood.

When they divided up to leave the house, John did a final sweep of the perimeter, ensuring all doors and windows were secure. The Stovalls traveled to the nearby Reindeer Creek Community Church in one of their vehicles that had survived the otherwise catastrophic fire. The Harrises traveled in the SUV with John driving and Ivy seated in the back with Harry and Candy. Arthur had grown to prefer the "look" of being chauffeured around but didn't want to be stuffed in the far back seat or with two other people tonight, even if those two other people were members of his family, so he begrudgingly sat up front with the driver he paid. John completely ignored the insult. He had more important things to keep front of mind.

"I aspire to own a car like this," Harry told Ivy.

She poked him in the ribs. "Study hard to take over your dad's business and you'll get the cars, too."

He clucked his tongue. "This isn't Dad's car. He's got some mechanic-looking work truck he takes out on the job sites."

She didn't hear the rest of his exposition about the type of truck Harry'd like to have for his site visits versus personal business. She was lost in her own thoughts, hoping materialism wasn't seeping into her opinion of John Knightley. *I was noticing my interest in him before I knew he had a ninety-thousand-dollar car.*

By the time they reached the church, she'd convinced herself she wasn't impressed with the vehicle. As he pulled it under the awning at the front of the building, where at least two chivalrous husbands were doing the same, he looked in the rearview mirror and locked eyes with Harry.

"Harry, you've got the ladies?"

"Yes, sir."

The door next to her clicked. Ivy reached for the handle, but it didn't open.

"I'll park this behemoth and check the perimeter," John said. "I'll join you in five."

Arthur had stepped out already and opened the back door for Candy behind him.

"My door didn't unlock," Ivy said.

"Can you pop the trunk so I can get the cookies?" Candy called as she stepped out beside Arthur.

Another click signaled the back was lifting. Harry started scooting toward his mom as John stepped out and opened Ivy's door.

"Oh, thank you. I think it was stuck," she said.

"Child locks," he said, taking her hand to help her down from the seat. "You can't open them from the inside."

"Oh, that seems…odd."

He winked. "It keeps clients from popping out of the vehicle without my permission."

Permission?

He hadn't released her hand yet and lowered his volume. "In the rush to get out of the house, I didn't get to speak to you. Everyone in the county knows Arthur and his family attend this church, so this is the event I have the most concern about this weekend. I'll look around before I come in to join you all, but I might be absent most of the evening. It's not for want of visiting with you. You look stunning and I know I'd rather be at your side than roaming the halls."

"Oh. Well. Thank… thank you."

Yes, stammer like an idiot.

"Ivy, would you carry this one for me?" Candy asked, stepping into view.

Ivy pulled her hand from John's and spun to accept a rectangular Tupperware container. "Got it."

Candy's grin spoke volumes.

"Is this all you need me to carry?" Ivy asked.

"Hang on. I've got a little bag of tongs and spatulas."

"Tongs and spatulas?" Ivy asked. It sounded crazily mundane.

"Yeah. People can use them to pick up cookies without using their fingers."

I guess that makes sense. "Shouldn't the church have those things in the fellowship hall?"

Candy reappeared with the aforementioned bag—a cloth, drawstring number that she laid on top of the Tupperware container. "It's always best to be prepared."

Ivy grinned at her. "Okay, Boss. Let's get you inside."

She glanced over her shoulder to see John had climbed back in the vehicle. He waited for them to lower the trunk, which she figured she was the one most free to handle. Balancing the container on her left hand and arm, she reached up for the button with her right hand. "We're clear?"

"Yep," Candy answered, standing back with a small stack of containers.

As Ivy looked back at the trunk, she saw three of the four Stovalls were closing in on the drive, but Lexie was lagging far behind with her crutches. *Oh man. He didn't drop the girls off at the door? Lexie has to hobble all the way across the parking lot? How stupid is that?*

Luckily, it looked like another teen in a long skirt and festive winter coat pranced up to poor Lexie to help her.

Ivy lowered the trunk with a press of the button under its lip and stepped back to look for Lexie again. "Hey, Harry, are you loaded down?"

"No. Mom shared all that with you."

"Could you jog out there and help Lexie?"

He stepped to her side and followed her gaze.

From where they stood, it looked like Lexie was standing off against the friend who'd approached her under the glow of parking lot lights. The new girl stood a few feet away from her, one arm bent so her hand rested on her hip and the other arm gestured in wide, jerking motions as she sang out Christmas carol words in screeching angry tones. Not all the words were audible by the church doors, but Ivy heard a few in clipped, bizarre rhythm. "It's Christmas time in the city" came at her like an angry rap flow instead of a pretty carol, as if the girl was using holiday lyrics to lecture Lexie.

"What's going on?" Harry asked.

"I don't know, but Lexie's not able to walk away from an altercation very easily. Mr. Stovall!"

"Hi there, Ivy, Harry," the man called, waving as he approached. He seemed oblivious to the strange, angry singing taking place behind him.

John leaned his head out the window. "Hey, could we get inside where it's *safe* and warm?"

Ivy nodded her head toward the parking lot. "Someone's yelling at Lexie. Could we help her out?"

"I'm going right now," Harry said. And, in fact, he took a step toward the sidewalk that split the landscaping feature along the drive when Lexie shrieked.

This garnered *almost* everyone's attention. Arthur had his head bent over his cell phone answering text messages. All other heads turned toward the argument in the parking lot, which wasn't an argument any longer.

Lexie was hopping backward with her crutches—away from a blur of gray motion.

Ivy blinked to clear her vision. Yes, the girl who had been yelling at Lexie was in the process of falling and sliding away from the scene. As if a foggy force engulfed and overpowered the girl, she fell backward onto the ice. As she skidded along it, her head contacted ice and asphalt with a *pop* they heard over the gasps under the awning.

Harry resumed moving again, this time running toward the girls.

John threw the SUV in gear and motored around the drive toward the scene.

Ivy spun to Candy. "You need to go inside with Arthur. Mrs. Stovall, can you take Lizzy inside, too? Lizzy, sweetie, here, can you take this for me?" Ivy was crossing the drive quickly, holding the container out to the girl. Lizzy had no choice but to accept. "Thank you, dear."

Ivy grabbed the bag from the top and pulled out a pair of tongs. Replacing the bag, she said, "Please get inside and call for an ambulance."

"An ambulance," Mr. Stovall repeated, as if trying to understand. "Yes, yes, an ambulance."

Ivy wasn't sure any of the people currently standing around gawking in shock at the violence they'd witnessed would be able to snap out of it and call for help. Unless Candy went into mothering mode. *Candy can take care of business if she thinks Lexie's still in danger out here.*

Ivy hurried out to the parking lot where Lexie already leaned into Harry, sobbing on his shoulder.

John had parked the SUV in the middle of the lane and the vehicle's headlights now illuminated him kneeling beside the motionless girl. As Ivy ran to him, he looked up with a defeated expression. "She's not breathing. There's no pulse."

In the shadow cast by their bodies, the growing puddle of blood under the girl's head looked black. Ivy struggled to pull her phone from her purse while juggling the tongs. "I'll get an ambulance. Can you do chest compressions?"

"Yeah, let me see if I can bring her back."

"Won't that make her head injury worse?" Harry asked. They heard terror in his voice.

"If we can't get her heart started, the head injury won't matter," John said, laying the girl's arms to her sides and setting his hands up for compressions on her breastbone. "Come on, my dear. Let's get you back here."

Ivy had her phone out by then and brought it to life. She hit the emergency call without going through the unlock feature.

"Nine-one-one, what's your emergency?" a calm voice asked.

"We have an accident at the Reindeer Creek Community Church on on on, what road is this?"

"Redemption Road," Lexie and Harry said together.

"Redemption Road," she spoke into the phone.

Chapter 13

Police arrived about two minutes ahead of the blaring ambulance. One of the officers took over chest compressions from John but none of them were able to revive the girl. Her name was Raya Kelter, and she was to be the soloist for the concert that night.

"I couldn't understand what she was saying," Lexie sniffled into her boyfriend's shoulder. He had replaced Harry at Lexie's side upon his arrival for the concert. Shortly after Zeke's arrival, though, police set up barriers at the church entrance to turn newcomers away. There'd be no Christmas concert at the Reindeer Creek Community Church this night.

"She sounded really mad. She was singing stuff about broken bells, but I couldn't understand anything else. And then." Lexie hiccupped and gulped back a sob. "Then she stopped yelling at me and looked at someone behind me like she was afraid of them."

Lexie hiccupped again. Her diaphragm was convulsing from the emotion, and she gulped for air. "And whoever it was ran past me and pushed her down. They flipping tackled her like a linebacker."

Ivy wished Lexie's parents would've sat with her for this interview. She wanted to talk to Harry about what he'd seen. Because this? This isn't what she'd seen. She hadn't seen anyone run past Lexie and tackle Raya. Of course, she couldn't tell the police officer that she'd seen a blurry cloud pull Raya to the pavement and crack her skull.

Because that sounds insane.

Unless that's what really happened.

I wonder what Harry saw. What made him hesitate when he was about to jog out there to help?

She looked out to the parking lot where John stood by his SUV with an officer. One of the officers had used chalk to draw an outline of Raya's body before the paramedics had placed her on a gurney and carried her away. When her parents arrived for the concert, the scene had been horrible and pathetic.

Terrible.

Ivy had found Candy sobbing in the church's poinsettia-laden sanctuary with young Lizzy Stovall trying to console her. Too many emotions were bubbling to the surface for her best friend, but at least she sought solace in a lovely place. She surrounded herself with the warmth of candlelit peacefulness while the emergency personnel shouted orders in the cold outside.

If someone was trying to break the heart of Arthur's family, that person was doing a good job of it tonight. *Psychological warfare. How awful that a young girl's life had to be snuffed out as part of the bargain.*

But something told Ivy the blur of darkness she'd seen attacking Raya had nothing to do with Arthur's business dealings. That smear of gray, substantive fog wasn't connected to vendettas against warring businesses as much as it was connected to hatefulness and a loss of goodness. The people in Reindeer Creek were slipping toward something unpleasant that had nothing to do with an architect's refusal to join a union.

As she braced for her turn to answer police questions, Ivy looked at the architect in question. He sat on a bench opposite hers in the wide church foyer, lost in his own world, obtuse and bordering on offensive with his demeanor. He exchanged text messages with someone who apparently had no interest in the tragedy taking place in Reindeer Creek.

He at least had the decency not to laugh out loud at his distraction. He had the forethought to cover his mouth when smiling at the phone in his hand, but the merry light in his eyes nearly sent Ivy into a rage.

"Ma'am?" the officer standing in front of her said.

"I'm sorry, what was that?"

"Could you tell me your name?" he repeated.

She shivered against the cold from the wide-open doors to her left. "Ivy Light."

"And what's your relationship to the deceased?"

"I don't know her." *And that seems a shame now, all things considered.*

"Are you related to the other girl involved in the altercation?"

"I'm not sure there was an altercation," Ivy said, cautiously. She didn't want any of the officers to think Lexie had participated in a fight leading up to Raya's death. "I was up here at the church door when I heard Lexie scream for help. I know Lexie Stovall because we're both staying at the Harris residence right now."

The officer nodded as he jotted down these notes. "You say Lexie screamed for help?"

"Yes."

"And what did you see?"

Here was the question she'd been dreading for the past hour. Nearly two. However long it had taken to get to this point. "I couldn't see very well because I was up here by the church door and Lexie was out there where Mr. Knightley's SUV is now."

Despite the crush of emergency vehicles, no one had asked John to move his Navigator. It was left there like a landmark for "the scene" they all kept referencing.

The officer stopped writing and studied her carefully. "You couldn't see very well." He spoke as if clarifying a statement he didn't believe.

"I couldn't. The parking lot lighting isn't great."

"What *did* you see?" he repeated.

Smart guy. He knows I didn't answer his question with all that chaff-and-redirect. He could work with the doctors I transcribe. "I saw blurs."

"Blurs?"

"Blurs." She paused, then clarified with, "Of motion." She paused again, then clarified further with, "As Raya fell on the ice."

"Blurs," he repeated, writing on his notepad. "Are those blurs what prompted you to take a pair of kitchen tongs to the scene?"

He knows I took that stupid pair of tongs out there? She swallowed against the worry building in her throat. "Tongs?" she asked, buying time.

The officer pointed with his pen to his right, toward the open doors, as if she could see what he referenced. "Mr. Knightley had a pair of tongs out there at the scene when we arrived."

Crap. He took those from me.

"He said you'd been carrying cookies and serving items into the church before running out to help. It seems odd you'd bring those things out to help a girl who'd fallen on the ice."

She nodded. *Yes, it does seem odd,* she agreed. But she wasn't going to say so.

"Could you tell me why you thought a pair of tongs would help—"

"Fine. I think I was going to rip them in two and stab whatever was threatening the girls," she blurted out.

He didn't write that in the notepad. "And what did you see threatening the girls?"

"I don't know. All I could see was blurs. Like I said, I couldn't see very well because I was up here by the church door and all I saw was blurs."

He tilted his head in Harry's direction. "Similar to Michael Harris' observation. A gray blur of motion."

She nodded, not willing to confirm anything else.

"Thank you, Ms. Light. And you're staying at the Harris residence?"

"Yes, sir."

"Thank you. If we have more questions, we can contact you there?"

"Yes."

He closed the notepad then and inhaled deeply. He looked out the doors toward the parking lot to release the breath. "It's a damn shame. Some coke-head probably, to move that fast. And now a young lady is dead right before Christmas." He looked back at Ivy. "I'm sorry your young friend is traumatized again. She's the one who just lost her home, isn't she?"

His shift into personhood caught her off guard. "Umm, yes. Her family was here for the concert tonight."

He shook his head. "It's a damn shame," he repeated. "We took up a collection at the department to get the gifts for the Stovall girls for Christmas and it didn't seem enough. And now this happens in front of them. What happened to her legs? I hadn't heard either of the girls had been injured in the fire."

"Oh, no, they got out of the house. But there was a freak accident with weird cold flooring at the Harris house last night and it blistered her feet."

Does he need to know all that? How much should I be telling him?

"Blisters from the cold?" he asked.

"Yeah, I didn't realize you can get burns from extreme cold the same as from heat. Like frostbite."

"Is she gonna be okay?"

"Yes." Ivy spoke with what she hoped was a sincere smile. "The doctor said it was mild. Bandaged her up as an abundance of caution. To keep infection at bay. The crutches are supposed to keep her from putting too much pressure on the wounds, but she *can* walk."

He nodded at this. "Sounds like she's going through a lot right now. Has she been to a therapist? Is she getting some help?"

If only.

"Not that I know of. I think the family could use a recommendation."

She was impressed with how smoothly—and quickly—he whisked a business card out of his breast pocket. "If they want to contact me, this is my direct information. Or if you want to reach out on their behalf. We can get her some help to walk her through everything. She's at a delicate age and this is a lot of difficult activity."

She read his name on the card. "Thank you, Officer Riley."

Chapter 14

They elected to stay home and relax on Sunday. They ordered groceries be delivered so they could make a pair of lasagnas and have a large, group meal with the two families. Ivy and John volunteered to clean up the kitchen so everyone could go back to their respective, placid places. Harry volunteered to go buy a Christmas tree for decorating but the group decided that would be a better activity for an evening later in the week.

Without lights.

Candy brought her silver bells ornament back to the kitchen to complete its cleaning. Her quiet countenance worried Ivy, but she offered excuses meant to set her guest at ease. "I have days of melancholy that come and go. But they go."

"And that's supposed to convince me not to worry about you?" Ivy asked.

"Yes. Hand me the red ribbon, would you?"

Ivy obeyed, watching in amazement how her best friend could create beauty while morose. It was as if she channeled some tortured Renaissance sculptor to bring a vintage ruin back to its former glory. She perfected the silver bells ornament to sparkling and reflecting stray light as if it had been crafted that very morning. She popped a dab of hot glue here and a dab there to affix the ribbon gracefully and reached for sprigs of greenery they'd bought the previous afternoon.

"It must have mistletoe," Candy said with a smile.

She affixed a poisonous sprig among the loops of ribbon and tied it off expertly. When she set it in the center of the island, she and Ivy stared at the work of art for a moment.

"That's amazing," Ivy breathed.

"Do I hand it to Lexie or to Marna?"

Ivy didn't hesitate. "Lexie."

"You think? If she bought it for her mom, would it be impactful for her mom to receive it?"

"I think this—right now, this would be impactful for Lexie to receive."

Chapter 15

When Ivy descended the wide staircase Monday morning, she found Arthur seated at the kitchen island with his cell phone pinging away and an amused smile on his face.

"Good morning. You look chipper today."

"Good morning. Yeah, I've decided today won't suck," he said. "I'm going into the office for a couple of my meetings to get out of this depressing place and it'll do me some good."

"Where's Candy? Still asleep?" She pulled a snowflake-speckled mug down from the cabinet and began pouring coffee from the pot someone had already made.

His cheeriness faded a degree. "Yeah, she's usually a downer after a church weekend coz of the little kids, you know? So, the past couple of nights have only made that more pronounced."

Ivy set the carafe back on the hot plate and turned to face him. *Time for this confrontation at last.*

"Sometimes, you sound incredibly callous and unfeeling. Are you telling me you're down here being chipper with your plans to escape to the office, all ready to make it a great day while you know for a fact your wife is upstairs thinking about the loss of her baby?"

He pocketed his cell phone and scowled at her. "You have no right to lecture me—"

"She's my best friend. I have every right. Are you going off to work with your bodyguard while Candy cries into her pillow after some random mugger killed one of your neighbors? A mugger who's still loose out there?"

"I can't be responsible for every criminal in Reindeer Creek."

"But you can be responsible for your family. She's not getting over her ordeal. She's still sad. You have to help her through this."

"The doctors told her carrying a child to term after forty was dangerous, but you know Candy. She's hard-headed. She tried it anyway. It's her own fault she lost a kid."

Ivy closed her eyes to tilt her head back a moment.

He took advantage of the break in the confrontation to drain the scotch from his morning beverage.

She let the stretch pull tension out of her voice so she could speak calmly. "Please tell me you've never said anything so cruel out loud before."

He scoffed as he set his highball heavily on the counter. "I've never said 'I told you so' to her, no. But I'm sure she realizes her situation is all her fault. I don't have to say it to her when I walk out of this situation. She knows." He scowled at the three ice cubes shifting in the glass now devoid of liquor. He watched a bead of condensation trail down the crystal's side as if its job was to rush to the countertop and join the ring forming there. "She knows," he repeated quietly.

Ivy's brows knit in a V of condemnation as she lowered her chin and fixed him in her judgmental gaze. *Did he just confirm he's walking out?* "Are you suggesting an immaculate conception here?"

"Don't be ridiculous," he snapped.

"Then I suppose you recognize how stupid you sound putting blame on her for the life and death of a child you should've loved, too?"

"I didn't say I didn't love my daughter. Don't go putting words in my mouth."

"Then what's the problem here?" Ivy asked. "Is it that you don't have enough love to stick around for your wife when she's still mourning the death of a child?"

"It's not that simple," he said, the spark of anger more an ember now.

Oh, God. He's not refuting it. He really did say he's walking out. "Then break it down for me, because I'm at a loss. What's so complex that you think I won't understand why you're planning to leave my best friend with a son in college and a still-broken heart? What's so complex that you think I won't understand you're about to rip her heart out a second time—"

"Okay, okay, you're making your point. You don't have to beat me over the head with it."

"Apparently, I do, because you haven't started making yours," she hissed.

"I fell in love with someone else."

They stared at each other for a second.

Two seconds.

Three seconds.

The shocking words hung on the air during that time, not quite echoing, not quite dissipating. Their power pulled the last ounce of energy from Arthur's arrogance. He deflated another degree while Ivy investigated his face, searching for—and finding—the regret behind not only the words, but also behind the truth of them.

Of the hundred questions flying through her brain, Ivy heard herself ask, "Who?"

"Meghan Temple. I don't know if you remember her from our college days at—"

"When?"

"What? What do you mean, when? I don't know when it happened. It was ages ago when I fell in love with her. Kinda one of those love-at-first-sight things where you see a girl across a crowded coffee—"

"Have you been having an affair with her or something all these years?"

"What? No. No, not at all. I'm not so crass as that. I'd forgotten about her some time ago. You know she left school the end of our freshman year for health reasons, and I started dating Candy. Meg looked me up on Facebook about eight months ago and we started private messaging—"

Ivy put a hand up, turning away from him. "I can't listen to this."

"What? I'm telling you this wasn't on purpose. Meg and I just kinda fell into talking and it just kinda rekindled these old feelings we used to have."

Ivy set her coffee mug on the counter by the sink, unsure she could prevent herself from throwing the scalding liquid in his face otherwise. She glanced toward the open archway while she spoke, ensuring no one was entering this space—no one was overhearing this terrible conversation.

"You've *got* to be kidding me. Are you that stupid? Have you met up with her in real life? Or is this online flirting making you believe you're back in love with some old flame?"

He frowned. "How dare you negate my feelings just because you don't have someone in your life."

She turned back to the island and placed both hands on its marble surface. "Don't assume you have any high ground here, mister. My private life has nothing to do with this. I asked you a question. How far has this homewrecker taken her advances on you?"

He startled at the question. "What?"

"Have you met her in person anywhere?"

"Well, no, not yet. She's coming to this area for Christmas. We're gonna meet at the old coffee shop where we first met—"

"You need to shut that down. I'm telling you right now, that woman isn't reaching out to visit an old friend online. She's got an agenda. She's coming here to tear up your family. She's coming here to get herself a husband. You. If she has to steal you from your family to do it, then that's—"

"You don't even remember Meghan. How can you say such a thing about a woman you don't know?"

Ivy took a deep breath and released it slowly. "Because I'm not the idiot in this room."

"You make it sound like adults can't talk to each other online. This is the twenty-first century, you know. Men and women conduct private conversations every day of the year in both business and personal arenas."

"I get that. But old flames don't reach out to married men and carry on private conversations with them without their wives' knowledge unless they have an agenda. Listen. If I were to find, oh, I don't know, Frank Dobles from our old study group, and reached out to see how he was doing, that would be a friendly gesture, right?

"But let's say he's married and has a couple kids. Do you know what would be appropriate at that point? It would be appropriate for me to keep my messages to him public. Public. Out in the open where he and his whole family can see all the things we're saying back and forth to one another. In fact, it would be appropriate for me to introduce myself to his wife to see if I have stuff in common with her, because a friend of Frank's should be a friend of mine.

"Do you see? What would be *in*appropriate would be for me to send a couple months of private messages back and forth to only Frank as if I didn't want his family to know I exist."

Arthur hung his head while listening. The man was being chastised, and he knew it. And he knew he deserved it.

116

"Sure. I get it," he said. "But we'd been texting for so long before I realized I was falling for her. I didn't know how to tell her—or if I wanted to tell her—that it was wrong."

Ivy squinted at him. "Does she know you're married?"

"Yes."

She shook her head. "That woman's a homewrecker. You gotta pull the plug."

"But I don't want to."

His confession, stated quietly so no judge or jury would hear it, would have elicited sympathy in a less moral woman.

"Are you telling me you *want* to leave your family?"

"No," he mumbled.

"Because that's what's going to come of this. The result of meeting up with a homewrecker—"

"I wish you'd stop calling her that."

"That's what she is. A homewrecker. A bimbo. A trollop who thinks it's okay to pursue another woman's husband. Nothing good will come of meeting with her in person. You will confuse yourself further and you'll ruin your marriage. I'm telling you, while you still have a chance to fix what's happening here, while you can still mend your heart and turn back to the woman who loves you, cut off communication with this interloper."

He snorted. "You make it sound like it's easy to turn off love."

"You're not in love with Meghan Temple. You're infatuated with the mystery and the intrigue of this chick from the past. Get over it."

He frowned at her. "You're acting pretty high and mighty for a guest in my home."

"I'm a guest in *Candy's* home. As are you at the moment. If you screw this up, she'll kick you to the curb and I'll put on some pointy boots to help her."

He scowled some more.

Before he could respond, footsteps on the staircase reached them. Ivy leaned back and turned to regather her coffee. She was sipping from it when John walked into the kitchen, rubbing his hands together. "Ready to go?"

When he saw Ivy, his face brightened, and his smile widened. "Good morning." He pointed at the coffee. "You like that flavor?"

She forced a smile for him. "It's very nice."

"Wow. Either that was a complete lie, or something's happened this morning. What's going on in here?"

"Nothing," Arthur groused. "I'm ready to go."

As the businessman strode past him with scowl and growl, John looked quizzically to Ivy.

She tried to hold her smile but couldn't. "Your boss and I have a difference of opinion on how to maintain a good family bond."

"Are you driving me to work or not?" Arthur boomed as he moved through the great room toward the garage.

"Getting my coffee," John called back as he stepped toward her. He lowered his voice to speak to her. "That sounds ominous."

He pulled a travel mug from the cabinet above her and looked to her eyes for answers she wasn't speaking out loud. "Should I have a family therapist brought in for these guys? Is something brewing between the Harris and Stovall clans? Because I thought yesterday was very healing."

She shook her head but then stopped. *What if the danger the past six months hasn't been from Arthur's competition but from Candy's?*

"Okay, that look is scaring the crap out of me," he said. "What are you thinking?"

"I wonder if your client should be Candy instead of Arthur."

He poured a measure of coffee into the travel mug to keep up at least part of the ruse while he nodded his head. "I'll contact a guy on the way to the office. Nick Alexander and Alvin Foley are with their families for the holiday now, but I have another associate I work with all the time. I haven't had a client for him to monitor since October, so he's available."

"Arthur won't agree with the reasoning I have here," she warned.

"I'm waiting!" Arthur shouted from the garage door.

John glanced to her as he replaced the carafe. "I'll call you as soon as I get him settled at his office." In the most intimate thing he'd done since meeting her in the boutique, he brought his hand up to her chin, brushing his fingers along her skin up to her cheek. "Be careful, then."

"I have access to all the kitchen utensils," she assured him with a wink.

Chapter 16

Ivy stood at the front window watching light flurries for a good five minutes after John drove away. She could lie to herself and say she was enjoying the spattering of snow on the wind, but the truth was she tossed the responsibility of protecting her best friend's heart from an idiotic husband.

Watching a neighbor drag a bin to the curb tickled the back of her mind until she realized that action meant it was trash day. Arthur should've taken out the trash. *But he probably leaves that for Candy to do because he's such an important businessman,* she scoffed inwardly.

Because she had no idea what time the sanitation workers would appear, she hurried into the kitchen and gathered up the bag from beneath the island. She'd left her tennis shoes upstairs, of course, but both Candy's winter coat and rubber boots were waiting in the coat closet near the garage door. With those squeezing her toes, she added the kitchen garbage to an already crowded trash can in the garage and pressed a button to raise the door.

Cold wind rushed in to greet her and she shivered against the winter mix. Hood up.

This will take two minutes and I can be back in where it's warm.

She tilted the heavy can onto its wheels and pulled it between her truck and the still snow-covered smart car in the driveway.

"Here, let me help you, Mrs. Harris!" a jovial voice called out.

She startled at a man in a huge red coat hurrying up the drive.

"Oh! You're not Candace."

"No, I'm Candy's friend. Just helping out this morning."

"Let me get that for you anyway," he said, still advancing. His disarming smile made up for startling her. "Looks like Arthur took off for work without doing his chores today."

Ivy refrained from pouncing on that opening. Instead, she said, "You must be one of the neighbors."

"I'm Robert Klauss. Live across the street."

She glanced at the three-story monstrosity with wrap-around porch and open iron gate. *Hunh. All these gates are open.*

"My house was up about a year before the Harrises started building so I've known them a while. You must be Ivy."

She grinned. "I must be. Candy mentioned you'd helped them get the lights up over here."

Mr. Klauss's smile faltered a bit then and he shook his head. "I tried to convince her to tone it down. You know she didn't decorate too much last year on account of just having lost the baby. She was pretty sad. This year, she went all out on the lights and the baubles and the music."

He parked the trash can at the end of the driveway as he spoke, straightening it parallel with the road. Pointing at the can, he said, "Please make sure someone takes this in before dusk. You don't want to leave this out past sundown."

As if that cryptic warning didn't bang around her brain, he easily continued the previous line of thought with, "She was so excited about decking the place out for the holiday and I couldn't dissuade her from it, so the best I could do was keep it contained to facing this way, this direction."

Ivy shrugged, pretending they were having a pleasant conversation about Christmas décor. "It is excessive, but if it makes her happy…"

Mr. Klauss shook his head some more, looking toward the back of the property, toward the trees. "I convinced her to keep it all on the front of the house. Facing the road and not directly disturbing the forest. Not disrupting the harmony of the woods and all that came before us."

Chapter 17

After an uncomfortable conversation with the widower from across the street, Ivy had deposited Candy's boots and coat back in the closet and returned to her coffee in the kitchen. Once again, she wanted to lie to herself and say she was merely contemplating some simple, pleasant tradition for the holiday. Maybe coming up with quick-and-easy breakfast foods to lift a best friend's spirits. Or she could admit to herself she mentally prepared for a phone call where John's voice and cadence would be close to her ear.

Which is the more productive and useful? Right. Breakfast for Candy.

Putting herself in motion was easier than thinking about a man she'd be walking away from in two weeks.

No time for girly romance.

She pulled a box of instant oatmeal packets from the pantry and opened it. Candy liked maple and brown sugar, so that's the one Ivy selected before replacing the box on the shelf.

See how girly romance turns out? Your husband strikes up a fantasy with some chick from the past while you mourn the loss of your child. Not worth it.

She made a simple breakfast of oatmeal and toast, coffee and orange juice, and was about to take the tray upstairs when Candy shuffled into the kitchen.

The two stared at each other for a second.

"Well, crap," Ivy said. "Umm. This is your breakfast in bed."

Candy grinned. "That's awesome. Can I eat it at the island?"

"Yeah. Park it."

Lexie shuffled in next. "Good morning," she yawned.

"Good morning. Should you be at school?" Candy asked.

"Mom said I could skip today since my feet hurt. She drove Lizzy in."

"And yet you're walking in here without your crutches," Ivy observed.

"My crutches make my armpits hurt. So, it's either my feet or my armpits. And I can stop my feet hurting if I sit still for a few minutes. Like now."

"I have something for you," Candy said.

"Me?"

"Have you eaten breakfast yet?" Ivy asked her.

"Yeah. Dad forces food on us in the mornings."

Ivy resisted the bizarre urge to tell the girl breakfast is the most important meal of the day. She figured it would be trite. She'd probably heard the phrase from her father a thousand times.

"He tells us it's the most important meal of the day," Lexie continued.

Ivy smiled to herself as she stared into the refrigerator, considering her own options for this oh-so-important foundation for Monday. If she wanted to get any transcribing work done on this vacation, she'd need something to focus her mind. Something more substantive than a cup of coffee.

"He's not wrong," Candy offered, pulling the gift from the cabinet.

Ivy glanced over at her friend, thinking parents must gain the ability to speak in colloquialisms when their children are born. *Maybe that's why I never developed the skill. Maybe that's why I never learned how to say the right things.*

As Candy turned with the small silver bells statue cupped in her hand, the air from the fridge reminded Ivy that she wasted its efficient cooling power. The motor must have cycled on at that moment because a puff of cold air seemed to breeze into her, cascading into her bones and chilling her marrow. She shivered as she closed the door. Oatmeal would be quick and easy for herself this morning, too.

Lexie gasped. "Oh my God. That looks just like—is that from my house? How did you get that? Did you guys go to that shop? Where did you get this?"

"Do you like it?" Candy asked, setting the gift on the island before her.

"It's beautiful!"

The women watched Lexie for a minute, aware that the girl transitioned through a series of emotions before them. She landed on joy-mixed-with-curiosity.

"How did you get this?"

"We looked around the property Saturday morning to see if there was anything we could salvage for you guys. I found this in—I found this and brought it home to clean."

Ivy wondered if Candy was going to say, "in the rubble." Maybe that phrasing was traumatizing for a child to hear right now. It was difficult to imagine your home as rubble or ruin.

"It's beautiful," Lexie repeated, this time with a breathy tone. "I wanted to give it to my mom for Christmas. It looks even better now, even without the handle on it."

She reached up to pull a necklace out of her shirt, revealing a loop for the pendant. The loop was a simple, silver circle—a bit too large in diameter to be worn as a ring—with a nub on its outer surface. She caught the circle and held it up for them to see the nub specifically.

"I broke it almost the minute I got it home. I felt so stupid. How was I gonna give my mom a broken gift? It cost me almost every dollar of allowance I'd saved. There was no way I could get anything else for her. So, I was stuck figuring out how to make it look like this was something special. Like I'd put effort into it, so she'd at least try to like it. I knew there was no way that weird shopkeeper at Under The Mistletoe was gonna refund my money or exchange it when I'd broken it. I couldn't tell her it was crappy workmanship or whatever. It was my fault. I'd ruined my chance to impress my mom and then the fire destroyed everything anyway."

Her voice trailed while she stared at the ornament between them.

She's wearing her mistake like an albatross around her neck.

"You made this look incredible. *This* is something my mom will like. Can I give it to her?"

The request for approval in Lexie's eyes touched Ivy's heart.

"Of course, you can," Candy said. "Whatever you want to do, this is yours."

Lexie stared at the ornament again and whispered, "thank you."

The sentiment was lovely, but odd. The girl seemed unhealthfully grateful for the gesture. It seemed strange that one simple present would carry so much weight, but then, Ivy hadn't lost every possession in a tragedy. Maybe this was a perfectly reasonable response to losing everything. She watched Lexie replacing the circle pendant in her shirt, re-hiding the broken part of the now beautiful bauble.

With Candy explaining that mistletoe is poisonous, Ivy returned to making breakfast for herself and jumped at her cell phone vibrating in her back pocket.

Probably John. Probably the conversation I can't have in front of Candy.

She grabbed the phone to see "Knightley Monitoring" spelled out above his phone number and pressed "accept call."

"Good morning again," she said.

"Good morning again," his rich voice poured into her. "Can you talk about your cryptic ideas from this morning?"

"Cryptic," she half-laughed. "I can do that in just a minute." She turned toward the two at the island and said, "Hey, I'm gonna take this call upstairs. I'll be back in a few."

Candy's face morphed into mischievous as she leaned toward Lexie. "I'm betting that's not work-related."

"What is it?" Lexie asked.

Ivy already walked through the doorway toward the stairs as she overheard—as she was supposed to overhear—Candy saying, "I bet that's Mr. Knightley checking in on her and we don't get to listen in."

"Okay, I'm headed upstairs so *busybodies* don't eavesdrop," she spoke to both John and the girls behind her. While John would surely understand she was teasing the people at the house, he probably wouldn't understand why, and she was okay with that.

She kept walking and talking. "I haven't eaten food yet so please don't ask me any tough questions."

"Tough questions require sustenance first?" he asked.

"Usually."

"Duly noted for the future. You at least drank the coffee? There's caffeine in your system by now, right?"

"Caffeine is on board," she said. "And thank goodness because this house is growing colder by the minute. Is it getting colder outside today?"

"Are you talking about the weather?" he asked.

"Yes, as a matter of fact, right now, I'm asking about the weather because I'm not sure the furnace in this house is keeping up with whatever the temperature is throwing at it from outside."

He chuckled. "To answer your question about the weather, no, the temperature isn't dropping today. The streets were clear all the way to Arthur's building. No traffic. No problems. We made it here in record time. I think everyone's taking the week before Christmas off. And that includes my brain. I forgot today's trash day in their subdivision. Can you knock on Harry's door and have him get the trash out to the curb?"

"Already solved," she said. "And the neighbor across the street helped and gave a creeptastic lecture about not upsetting the spirit of Reindeer Creek with our holiday decorations."

"I don't know what that means. But I appreciate you helping keep things on track there."

Ivy had reached her room at this point and closed the door behind her. She walked to the first bay window and opened the curtain as she spoke. "All right. I'll throw on more layers and cope.

"Now, for my cryptic idea, I think we should consider Arthur might not be the target of harassment in this family. It might be Candy. Did someone actually threaten them this summer or did Arthur *imagine* someone might threaten them? Is all this security in place because of an actual threat he received? Or because he got paranoid?"

John laughed again. "Arthur can be paranoid at times, but they did get a series of untraceable letters at this office. They looked like they were the real deal. And they were threatening Arthur's business first, which the insurance company took seriously. Tell me why you think Candy's in danger. What's going on at the house?"

Ivy stared at the snowy ground, watching the off-blue cast smearing with purpling sparkles in the morning light. Lacy shadows from the tree line stretched across lawn, reaching for the house, promising to prevent the snow from melting into mud and brown-grass ugliness before Christmas. Promising to keep it picturesque for the holiday.

"Just my overactive imagination, I guess. I started to worry about someone Arthur's bringing into the picture. That idiot's trying to hook up with an old flame."

Saying it out loud made her blood move faster. Her internal temperature accommodated the cooler air she'd been complaining about moments before.

"I'm sure I didn't hear you right. Say that again?"

"Yeah, he admitted it to me this morning. This chick we all knew in college. Well, our freshman year of college. Meghan Temple. She was only there our freshman year because she got sick and had to go home. Anyway, I guess she and Arthur were a thing briefly that year. After she left, he and Candy started dating and that became permanent. But last year, Meghan found Arthur online and started up a relationship. Even though she knows he's married. Now this idiot thinks he wants to meet up with her somewhere over the holiday."

John was silent for a minute.

"Are you still there?" she asked.

"Yeah, sorry, give me just a second. I've found her. Looks like Meghan B. Temple left college because she was pregnant. She looks different these days as an older lady and, man, she looks really familiar now. Like I've seen her somewhere."

Ivy chuckled. "I think I've heard that line."

"Hunh. Maybe that's where I've seen her. When we were at that shop."

"Omigosh!" Ivy remembered then. "That shopkeeper seemed familiar to me when I was in there, but I didn't know why. It makes sense now. I knew Meghan our freshman year but that was, what, twenty-six, twenty-seven years ago?"

"While I refuse to believe you've been out of school twenty-someodd years, I'll not let that distract us. If we think Arthur's side chick works at Under The Mistletoe, I can look up to see if she's a manager or what level of…hang on…lemme get into their records."

This made sense to Ivy. "See just how stalkery she is? Did she buy that shop nearby or is she there as part-time help to weasel her way into Arthur's life?"

"Exactly…oh, man."

"What?"

"Oh, man," he repeated, somewhat wistfully.

"What? You sound like I just ruined your whole week. What's wrong?"

"Ivy, this looks bad. Her baby?"

"Yeah?" *I know exactly what he's about to say.*

"This man grew up looking exactly like Arthur Harris. He's the spitting image of Michael Harris. But without Candy's smile."

It was Ivy's turn to be silent.

I wonder if Arthur knows this part. Did he leave this part out because he knew I'd throttle him?

"I wonder if Arthur knows this part," John breathed into the phone.

Chapter 18

The call with Ivy made John's left eye twitch. He wanted to punch his client for blatant stupidity, but he knew Arthur Harris was merely one of those misled businessmen looking for his midlife crisis point. He glanced to the phone bank on the secretary's desk to see Arthur was still on his conference call. The secretary smiled sweetly at him.

"How much longer?" John asked.

"This call is scheduled until 9:30. Then he has a zoom with the commissioners from 9:30 to 11:00."

John nodded and put on the charm. "Business doesn't get to take a holiday."

She giggled and twirled her blond hair around her well-manicured index finger. "Nope."

"I'll be in the lobby if he should need me before his calls are done."

He stepped out the glass door with "Harris Design/Build" emblazoned on it and pressed his buddy's name on the cell phone.

"Knightley. Please tell me you're not calling me to action," a man's voice intoned.

"I need your help out here," John said.

"Hang on a second."

The sounds of children laughing and shrieking at one another in the background intensified as Jack

Henry moved the phone away from his shouting, "Guys, Uncle Jack's got a phone call here."

John distinctly heard a young voice shout, "My turn! My turn!" Then an adult announced, "Donuts for everyone!"

Sugar sounds like the last thing that crowd needs.

The tones of *Rudolph the Red-nosed Reindeer* assaulted him like the Doppler Effect as his colleague moved through what must have been an early gathering of excited kids until the sound of a door clicking closed preceded Jack clearing his throat. "Okay. Let's hear what you've got going on."

"I can take you away from whatever that chaos is," John said into the phone.

Jack laughed on the other end of the connection. "While I appreciate the sentiment, this isn't as bad as it must sound on your side of the continent."

"I'm only in Kansas," John said.

"Oh. For some reason, I thought you were out in Washington State."

"Nah. Somewhere near the Kansas-Missouri border. But this client I've been guarding the past six months has a situation developing."

"Got himself more trouble than winning jobs away from the local union-backed contractors?"

"Ah, you remember," John said.

"Nick filled me in on some of the particulars. Just in case."

John chuckled to himself. *I work with the best guys in the business.* "Well, Nick was more in tune to this dude than I was."

"How's that?"

"This guy." John glanced around the lobby to make sure no open doors offered audiences to his end of the conversation. "He's been getting ready to step out on his wife, so there's a side chick who may or may not already be in the picture."

"Crazy side chick?"

"High potential for crazy, yes. I just learned of her. And of her adult son who might be interested in challenging the family for a piece of the family business, if you catch my drift."

"Geez. Great time of year for a showdown. Can't people time their vendettas better?"

"I'll be running a more thorough background check on the woman and her son when we get off this call. But if I want to protect the wife and families at the house, I need someone to keep up with the businessman."

"Families, plural?"

"Yeah, there was a house fire down the street so Candy—Mrs. Harris—took in the family. Four people. They're living in the downstairs apartment until they can get things squared away with insurance and can go to a family down in Mississippi, I think, while they rebuild. Mississippi or Louisiana."

"Dude, do you hear yourself? There was a housefire down the street from your client?"

"Yeah, I looked into it. Christmas tree went up in the house. Not related to my guy. It *might* have been arson, but if it was, it was for the insurance."

"You hope. Man, doesn't anyone remember what this season is about? These people keep attracting bad stuff to themselves. This is supposed to be the time of year to attract good."

It was a noble sentiment for his freelance muscle to share, but John agreed.

"Yeah. I'm regretting sending Nick home for the holidays. But he has a new kid and I thought I could keep Arthur under my watch for Christmas. He's not supposed to be coming into the office at all this week. He's supposed to be doing all his work from the home office. But this side chick action kinda explains his desire to get out. Ivy thinks he's setting up a meeting with the woman any day now."

Jack began to chuckle into the phone.

"What?" John asked.

"Tell me about Ivy."

Jerk. "Do you want the work or not?"

"Where do you need me to be and when?" Jack asked.

"I need you to be in Reindeer Creek, Kansas, as soon as you can get here. I plan to put you on Arthur Harris while I stay on the families."

"I'm good with that. What else are you forgetting to tell me?"

"Mmm. The son here invited one of his professors to come in. An Adam Thackery arrives either today or tomorrow, depending on his ability to meet a deadline back at the university. Apparently, his whole family's down with one of the Covid variants—mother, couple of sisters, an aunt, I don't know how many people he was going to see—so he was planning to stay at the university and Harry's earning karma points instead."

"The kid's smart," Jack said. "Bring the professor home for Christmas dinner with the family and he gets an A for the semester."

"Probably. But Alvin checked this guy out and he's harmless. The only other *weird* thing is some huge wolf came off the prairie the other night and walked right into the house."

"Holy Christ. A wolf?"

"It tried to attack one of the teens in the house," John continued. "So, if you can bring a hunting rifle, that would be great."

"They're not gonna let me bring a hunting rifle on a plane, no matter how many permits I flash at them. But a wolf? Surely, that's not part of the threats your guy's been getting the past six months?"

"Yeah. I can't imagine that's a tactic the union guys use to intimidate their competition, but it was noteworthy."

"Noteworthy's a fact," Jack agreed. "What did you tell the police?"

"The truth. A wolf got in."

Jack laughed. "I bet that went over real well."

"The Leos around here have been kinda busy with other problems. Some mugger slipped away after killing a parishioner Saturday night."

"You did *not* just drop that statement as an afterthought. Do you hear yourself? These things are adding up to something very uncool. When did you send Nick on vacation?"

"A couple of days ago. Friday. I was on my way back from leaving him at the airport when I ran into Ivy coming into town. But when Nick comes back after the first of the year, you can get back to your life."

"I might not agree to that. It sounds like you're in the middle of a war that your client doesn't realize he started. But, hey, would Nick be able to tell me about Ivy?"

"I'm hanging up now."

Chapter 19

John was in the middle of performing a deep background check on the financially unstable Meghan Temple and her unemployed adult son when Ivy called his cell phone again.

"This is a treat. How can I help you?"

"Hey," she said. "There's a tree trimming service here at the house claiming Arthur hired them."

"Oh. I don't like the sound of that."

"Agreed. Candy let them get to work on the trees out back. You know, the trees that line the back of the property? But I don't like the story they gave us. Something about keeping the trees tidy so the city can't have an excuse to rezone the protected land adjacent the property. It sounds very sus."

John closed his eyes for a minute, trying to recall anything he knew about arboriculture.

"I mean, the only time you trim a tree in the dead of winter is when an ice storm is on the horizon, right?" she continued. "To keep potential weight from downing limbs and killing the tree or taking out power lines. There are no power lines back there."

Ivy couldn't see him, but John nodded at this logic. "Did she let them in the house?"

"No."

"Good. What's the name of the company? Can you see their truck from inside?"

"I have their business card in my hand," she said.
"God, you're good at this. Go ahead."

"It's Roots Tree Service. The guy on the card is Dash Heggs and he acted like he knew what he was talking about. But, ya know how you just a get a feeling from some people? There was something odd about him. Something plastic or fake. Even his beard looked like those old Halloween masks from when we were kids. And there's no website listed on his business card."

"Roots? Like the roots of a tree?" he clarified. He wasn't ignoring the odd description of Dash Heggs, but he wasn't finding a tree service by the name of "Boots." He must have misheard her over the cell phone connection.

"Yeah."

"Not very original," he muttered as he typed the correct word into the search field on his laptop.

"The phone number isn't a Kansas number, either," she offered.

"Is there a logo on the card?"

"Yeah. Sort of. It's a tree."

"I'm looking at a website here for a Roots Tree Service out of Florida and it has an elm tree for a logo," he said.

"An elm tree in Florida?" she asked.

"Yeah, I think that's odd, too. Then doing business up here in Kansas makes it strange. What's the phone number?"

"Three five two, three three three, five two five two."

"Not very original. That's a Florida phone number, if it's real." He already rose from his desk, closing the laptop and moving toward the secretary's desk. *I never should've sent Nick home.* "Lock all the doors. I'm pulling Arthur out of his meetings and we're on our way back now. Don't open the door for them again. Are the Stovalls downstairs?"

"Lexie is. Marna drove Lizzy to school before she went to her office and Leland went to his."

"Check on Lexie and that exterior door to the garage. Do you know about the door off the kitchen pantry? That delivery—"

"Got it. We'll tighten everything up here."

"Don't hesitate to call the police if you doubt anything happening out there. Bring everyone into one room together away from windows where none of the workers can see you."

"Got it. I'll hand out cookie scribes."

"Ivy."

"Don't worry. Candy and I know how to kick ass."

*****

Ivy deposited her phone in her pocket and turned to Candy to suggest they get Lexie from the basement when the front doorbell sounded. "Don't answer it," she said.

"Really?" Candy said. "John thinks these guys are a danger, too?"

"Neither of us can verify who these guys are yet."

Harry jumped from the last step of the staircase and rushed past the kitchen while they were talking. His socks slid to a stop at the front double doors, but he didn't pause there as Ivy expected him to do.

She continued, "Until John calls back with information or returns with—Harry!"

The young man flung open the front door to a blast of cold air and a man's grumpy greeting, "I went to the wrong house first."

"Welcome to The Harris Chalet, Dr. Thackery. Come on in."

"That kid's gonna give me a heart attack," Ivy muttered, trailing Candy into the expansive foyer.

"Bring your guest in and close the door before Aunt Ivy collapses," Candy said. "Welcome, Mr. Thackery. It's great to have you join us for Christmas. Please don't mind any stray dust. We had some contractors in Saturday and we didn't quite get all cleaned up from that."

The man stepped into the house with a swirl of cold air and leftover clove cigar. He stamped nonexistent snow from his ankle-high boots on the mat before the door and set a carry-on suitcase in the immediate entryway.

Good tripping hazard.

"I'm Candace Harris, Michael's mom."

"A pleasure, Ma'am. Thank you for inviting me." He began unwrapping a long cashmere scarf from 'round his neck.

"Harry, can you get his coat for him?"

"Yeah, yeah, let him get in the door, Mom."

"What's going on up here?" Lexie asked, hobbling from the basement stairs.

Ivy motioned her forward. "More company for Christmas."

"I guess. I keep hearing the doorbell."

"Mmm. We have tree trimmers out back that we're keeping an eye on. Now we have a new guest."

Lexie glanced toward the back windows before bringing her attention to the small group near the door again. "Should people be trimming the trees on protected land?"

"Not at all," Ivy said. "But we're letting that play out until Mr. Knightley gets back with Arthur and ammunition."

"Ammunition?" Professor Thackery startled, handing his faux leather driving gloves to Harry.

Harry waved the gloves as if dismissing Ivy's sarcasm for him. "You might remember I told you my dad's paranoid? Well, my Aunt Ivy's paranoid, too."

Ivy extended her hand to greet Professor Thackery more politely. *Wow. An older Remington Steele.* "You're only paranoid if they're *not* out to get you, right? It's a pleasure to meet you, Dr. Thackery. May I call you Adam?"

The man lost a hint of his stateliness as he smiled patiently at her. "Of course. Please do. I hope it's all right that I parked behind that gas-guzzling monstrosity of a truck out there in the driveway. Does that carbon nightmare belong to these workers maiming the forest? Will I need to move my car for them to leave?"

Ivy almost laughed out loud. *Oh, this holiday managed to bump up a notch in the wacky category.*

"You won't need to move your car," Candy assured him.

"I want to see these tree trimmers," Lexie said quietly.

"That's probably not a great idea," Ivy said, remembering John's instructions. "We should stay away from the windows."

"Why are we staying away from the windows?" the professor asked.

"Because Aunt Ivy's paranoid," Harry reminded them.

"Because we don't want to appear rude," Candy supplied.

"Because it's best to hide our numbers," Harry quipped.

Ivy punched his arm lightly. "You're being impertinent today, aren't you?"

"Really, I want to see them," Lexie said, hobbling toward the back of the great room, toward the large windows that overlooked the backyard and frozen pond. "I don't think they should be messing with the trees back there."

Ivy recognized the girl's level of concern and followed her to the large, clean glass. "They're just trimming things up to be tidy. Did you know Mr. Harris is working to keep the county commissioners from rezoning the land back there? He wants to make sure no one takes away its protected status, so keeping the trees neat and tidy keeps the authorities happy."

Lexie offered her a dubious glance. "That sounds made up."

Ivy grimaced. "Yeah, it sounded sus when the dude said it on the front porch. But it kinda makes sense. Arthur really is trying to keep the land protected back there."

Lexie nodded at that.

Did I finally say the right thing?

"He looks like one of Mrs. Harris' snowman gnomes," Lexie said. "There's no way he can climb that ladder."

"Lexie," Candy scoffed gently as she approached. "That's not very kind."

"Look, I'm not trying to be mean about it," Lexie said. "It's just a fact. He's wearing the same green pants and green puffy vest thing as your snowman dude by the mailbox."

Ivy considered this. She'd not paid as much attention to the individual lawn ornaments as Lexie had, obviously, but the poor guy carrying an unwieldy aluminum ladder to the back of the property looked like the typical Christmas gnome.

But life-size.

"Notice how his hair sticks out from under his cap," Lexie said. She nervously rubbed at the silver circle she'd pulled from beneath her shirt while she spoke. "Isn't it just like the gnome's hair? It even has a ceramic look to it. Like the wind could whip through the trees and that hair won't move a bit."

"The cap certainly won't blow off," Ivy muttered. She was starting to agree with Lexie. The guy who'd introduced himself as Dash Heggs looked like he'd stepped away from someone's lawn display and grown to human size to come work on the tree line behind the Harris house.

The fellow leaned the metal ladder against a tree and shook it as if testing its security. They were far enough from the scene and insulated enough by the thick glass they couldn't hear the metal clanking of a construction ladder, but Ivy imagined it anyway, complete with heavy bungee cord clunking against its legs. His partner handed him what looked like a battery-powered chainsaw. If the thing could cut through more than one branch, she'd be surprised.

She clearly heard the click of the coat closet door as Harry finished depositing Professor Thackery's outerwear and listened for their footsteps to join them. *John would have a fit if he could see this. Each one of us lined up here at the window, exactly where he told me not to have us.* Of course, John hadn't indicated he was prone to fits of anger when his orders were balked. He rolled with the punches nicely. He'd probably smirk at her with that way too sexy mouth.

Enough of that thinking.

The snowman-gnome worker had made it half-way up the ladder and stopped. Because her attention was focused on Mr. Heggs, his plastic-looking hair, and the diminutive chainsaw he now fired up with a whine-and-whir, she lost track of his partner. Would that fellow try to approach the front door next? Try to breach the stronghold?

She wanted to move everyone to an interior room. "Maybe we should all—"

Lexie shrieked as a blur of gray wintery mix slammed into the worker outside. Both ladder and chunky gnome crashed over in a fast-motion slam to the ground.

Snow exploded along the footprint of the falling ladder. And as stark red sprayed up from the chainsaw's grinding whir-and-scream against bone and metal, Ivy grabbed Lexie and spun her away from the gore. She buried the child's face in her shoulder, away from the horrifying thrashing that ended long before the crimson shower.

Chapter 20

Ivy sat on the lowest step emptying into the Harris great room, watching activity and hearing voices—processing none of the whirl. She'd never seen a person die prior to this trip to Reindeer Creek and now she'd seen two violent deaths in less than forty-eight hours. It caused a chill to grip her spine; grip and squeeze her vertebrae.

Officer Ben Riley walked toward her and smoothly took a seat on the step beside her. He waited a moment before he spoke. "I don't want to ask what you saw. Don't want to make you relive this morning's events. But I have to write down what you remember."

She nodded. *That makes sense. Full report and all.*

Without waiting for him to formally ask, she volunteered, "I saw Mr. Heggs climb half-way up the ladder, start up the chainsaw, and then fall over with a gust of wind." She gulped, seeing the blur of snow and ice as a gray fog of winter slamming into the heavy man. "But I think he fell onto the chainsaw. I think the ladder trapped him. I didn't see—I didn't see how that part happened. I was shielding Lexie's eyes then."

She was aware that the officer pulled his notepad from his belt and jotted down her recounting of events. The scribbling of his pen seemed normal amid the insanity she'd witnessed. *Are normal things going to happen again? Are they allowed to happen again?*

"Mr. Heggs seemed like a pretty heavy-set fellow for a gust of wind to push him over," Officer Riley said carefully.

She sighed. "I agree. He seemed a bit heavy for going up a ladder. But who I am to judge anyone's physical fitness?" She paused, thinking that the officer probably wanted something better than wind to explain how the man at the back of the Harris property fell off a ladder onto an active chainsaw.

"Who am I to judge who can and can't balance properly on construction equipment?" she asked quietly. "If he couldn't maintain balance while wielding dangerous tools, he shouldn't have been assigned that task. He should've been assigned a different job for his company."

"Do you think this should be an OSHA investigation now?" he asked.

"It was an OSHA investigation the minute he propped a ladder against the tree without securing it."

"I have to agree," he said, closing the notepad again. "Thank you for shielding Lexie from it. The poor girl needs a break. She needs something normal. Something peaceful."

"She needs Christmas," Ivy practically whispered.

"What's that?"

"I was coming here to join my best friend for Christmas. It was supposed to be jolly and fun, peaceful and restorative." She let the descriptors fade rather than pull the detective into the idea of what therapy she'd planned to bring to Candy. "Instead..."

Officer Ben Riley put a hand on her shoulder and offered a comforting squeeze. "You're taking on a monstrous amount of stress, Miss Light. I wish you'd see the comfort you bring to that young lady. I interviewed her a moment ago and it's obvious she looks to you as a role model. She sees you as a friend and confidante. You're making a good and positive difference for her by being here.

"You may have come to Reindeer Creek for a jolly holiday, and that may yet be in the cards once these past few days of stress are in the rearview, but you've also come to Reindeer Creek for a good and positive purpose. I can see it."

It was nice of him to say such a thing. She appreciated the kindness. The pep talk, if that's what it was.

"Thank you," she said.

Approaching tactical boots saved her from trying to find anything else to say. She looked up to see John Knightley standing before them.

"Are you done interviewing Miss Light?" he asked.

"Yes, I think I've gathered all—"

"Great. Professor Thackery wanted to ask a few questions about Reindeer Creek law enforcement. Can you help him?" While John spoke to the officer, he held his hand out to Ivy. He assisted her up from the step.

"Ah, sure, yeah, I can help the professor. Where'd he wander off to?" Officer Riley asked as he rose to his feet beside her.

"He's back there by the window, watching them shovel up the—the snow."

Ivy wondered if he was about to say, "the mess." He'd caught himself and changed it rather than bring the blood and gore to mind. *Too late*.

As Officer Riley wandered toward the back of the great room, John led Ivy into the kitchen. "I can't express how relieved I am to find none of you ran out to help the injured worker."

"Oh. That's not quite what I expected you to say."

"It's the truth. When we rounded the bend to see the flashing emergency lights were at this house? I can't tell you—I don't think I can describe what happened in my stomach. A thousand scenes flashed through my brain. Did anyone tell you I left Arthur in the car to run in here to check on you? All. You all?"

She almost laughed. "Child locks on the doors?"

"Ah, yes. He was stuck for a bit. But he's resourceful. I'm incredibly thankful you kept everyone in the house. Harry said he wanted to go out there. Was putting on his boots and you stopped him."

"Where are we going?" she asked. It seemed odd that he'd walked her to the pantry of all things.

"I want to show you this hallway."

"Hallway." She said the word with enough disbelief that he chuckled.

"Yes, the hallway that can serve as an escape route if you need it. This is the first time you've visited the house since they finished it, right?"

"Yeah, but Candy gave me a tour Saturday morning."

"Did she show you this hall off the kitchen?" he asked.

"The pantry?"

He opened the pantry door, which, truth be told, led to an impressive room. But she wouldn't call it a hallway. This was an overachieving closet, which Candy had disappeared into multiple times already this holiday and emerged with any number of delicacies. *A magical holiday portal.*

"See that wallpaper back there?" he asked.

The wallpaper had caught her eye the first time she saw it; when Candy had shown her around the house. The scene of old-fashioned desserts on cooling racks didn't seem like Arthur's style, but it reminded her of Candy's parents' house when they were kids.

Mrs. Kane had always had pies and cakes and homemade breads cooling on racks and windowsills like it was the 1950s or even prairie days. Ivy figured the wallpaper in the pantry was a reminder of a childhood filled with mouth-watering baked goods.

"That's a door," John said.

He led her all the way into the pantry and closed the kitchen door behind them.

Dark.

He flipped the light switch to their right and a soft, buttery light shone down from an old-fashioned cast-iron lantern. He stepped the few paces past rows of foodstuffs and canned goods to the wallpaper of childhood memories and lifted a latch that, until that moment, had looked like part of a metal cooling rack.

Well, whaddya know? Candy's got a secret passageway in her house.

The door swung into a concrete hallway with track lighting along the baseboard.

"They have groceries delivered through here, so it's not a big secret. But it's also not easy to identify unless you already know it's here."

He led her into the wide hall where an unfinished cabinet displayed its cleaning supplies. Next to it, a mop and broom awaited their future service. She could easily see the deadbolt and handle for the door at the other end of the hallway, which was only about twelve feet away. She wondered what was on the other side of the wall.

He tapped on the wall adjacent the unfinished cabinet. "The garden shed is on the other side of here."

She grinned. "I was just wondering."

He leaned against the unfinished cabinet, partially cloaked in shadow from the door that still stood open beside them. "I spoke with Adam Thackery, Harry's professor friend, about the accident. Poor guy's rethinking his vacation plans."

"Yeah, he walked in, took off his coat, and witnessed a horrible accident."

"He told me something strange," John said.

"Given what happened out back, there are only strange things to tell."

He nodded at the truth of her statement. "That's a fact. He told me about this gust of wind that he could literally see."

"Mmm. Same here."

"You saw it, too?"

"Yeah. Gray, snowy wind. Like the wind had a fogginess to it." She refused to say, *like the foggy wind we saw attack Raya Kelter Saturday*. Instead, she finished with, "That's what knocked Mr. Heggs and his ladder over."

John nodded. "That's what Thackery described. But he also mentioned Lexie."

"Poor Lexie. She saw it happen." *Again.*

"Does she have a silver pendant around her neck?" he asked.

"Oh. I didn't expect that question. Yeah, she has this silver ring on a chain. It broke off that ornament she was gonna give her mom for Christmas."

John stared at her for a moment, obviously processing the extra information she'd just volunteered. "That makes what Thackery told me even stranger."

"I'm starting to get freaked out. You wanna just say it?"

"He told me she was fidgeting with a silver pendant and invoking the spirit of the protected land."

Ivy caught herself about to laugh at that. "Invoking what?" *These guys could be channeling Mr. Klauss!*

"Yeah, it sounds strange, but I'm starting to think about this some more. When Thackery was telling it, it sounded like psychic foo-foo business. But now that I know the ring she's got isn't so much a pendant as it is part of the silver bells thing Candy found in the rubble—" He let his thought trail for a second before seeming to make a decision. "Maybe there's something we need to look into. He told me metals are good for holding spirits and communicating with spirits—good and bad ones."

This has officially become my worst Christmas on record.

"He said silver is particularly powerful," John continued. "And it's known for being an especially good conduit for bad spirits."

"It's also good for killing werewolves," she suggested. She wasn't trying to mock his sincerity but wanted to pull the conversation back to reality. This was Kansas, middle of the United States, in the year 2024. Were bad spirits supposed to be haunting new subdivisions?

He offered one of those half-smiles that made her insides flop.

"You tease me, but listen to this," he said. "What if that wolf targeted Lexie because she has that silver thing like a talisman around her neck? And what if that other wolf came to the driveway Saturday because Candy had the silver bells in her bag? And what if something attacked Lexie and Raya Saturday night because, again, Lexie's got that thing around her neck?"

"And some strange wind attacked a stranger we don't know out back because both the bells and the ring are in the house today?" she asked dubiously.

He shrugged. "I think it's worth going back to Under The Mistletoe to not only check out who we think is Meghan Temple, but also to ask the weird shopkeeper about the statue she sold to a teenager. Did Candy get the thing cleaned up? Is it presentable again? We could take it to show the woman what we're talking about."

Ivy nodded. "Candy not only cleaned it, she added some ribbon and stuff to it to make it stunning. She already gave it back to Lexie, though. We'd need to ask Lexie if we could borrow it."

"I think it's worth it to ask that favor. Lexie would probably let us if we explained we're concerned for her safety."

Ivy thought it might be pre-emptive to tell the girl such a shocking thing, but she was willing to go along with asking "the shopkeeper" some questions. *Why not add some accusations of insanity from the local vendors while on this vacation?*

"And speaking of Lexie, Candy called her parents a bit ago," he said. "Her mom can't get away from the office yet but Leland's on his way back here now."

Ivy caught herself almost laughing again. "They'll have nowhere to park."

He offered her a puzzled look.

"The garage is full, right? And the driveway is packed with cars and now emergency vehicles line the street out front. But I guess the ambulance and police cars all leave pretty soon. They show up, clean the mess, then leave."

"Are you in shock?" he asked.

She did laugh now. "Probably. I just watched a man get hacked up by his own—"

She let the thought trail away. *Wrong thing to say.*

Unfolding his arms from across his chest, he said, "That sounds like a good reason to be in shock. But it's disappointing."

"Disappointing?"

Well, crap. Does he think I'm weak or something?

"Yes. You see, I had this great plan worked out. I'd thought, while there were police and well-trained civil servants out there protecting the Harrises, I could pull you away from all the people and activity and reminders of gruesome things. I thought I could bring you into a quiet space under the false pretense of showing you this escape route out of the house, and then pull you into my arms."

He proceeded to reach both hands out to her arms and bring her into his personal space while he spoke.

False pretense? What?

"And if you didn't get mad at me for being so forward, maybe I could even get away with holding you in this safe, quiet space."

No kidding.

He enveloped her in the strength and warmth of his arms, holding her close, letting her conform to the shape of him. She relaxed into this hold. Her muscles melted out of tension and into serenity with her cheek to his shoulder and her palms resting against his chest. She could press away from him if she chose to but why on Earth would she choose that? This was comforting.

Pleasant.

Home.

"What disappoints me is I wanted to hold you since I met you in that boutique Friday evening. But I didn't want to take advantage of my sweet Ivy in a moment of distress. So let me pull the anxiety out of you for a moment now."

She closed her eyes.

"Let me settle and calm your nerves for you now."

She breathed in the nutmeg and musk captured in the fabric beneath her cheek.

"Let me hold you for pedestrian purposes now." He kissed her forehead. "And I'll hold you again some other evening when there's no more anxiety. Just calm and Christmas lights some other evening."

She sighed into the thought. *That sounds idyllic.*

Chapter 21

Tuesday brought complete disappointment. While Lexie allowed them to borrow the silver bells to take back to Under The Mistletoe, they arrived at the shop that afternoon to find its parking lot empty of cars and full of snowdrifts and potholes. The shop itself was boarded up with a sign on the door declaring the property condemned.

"You've got to be kidding," Ivy said, stamping her feet on the faded, green bristle mat tossed by wind outside the front door. The mat looked as if it had been overused and nearly torn to shreds in the past four days.

John cupped his gloved hand against a window, trying to ascertain movement or life inside the shop. "Now I'm inclined to ask the professor to do some research," he said.

"Professor Thackery? Why would he have insight about Arthur's potential side chick's creepy store?"

John smiled. "It sounds convoluted and crazy, doesn't it?"

He walked to the side of the shop and grimaced at the dumpster brimming with mildewed Christmas tapestries, splintered and faded giant nutcrackers, and broken fiber optic trees. "This stuff looks like it's been in someone's attic for a decade."

He returned to her saying, "This whole place looks like it's been condemned for years. Look how dilapidated this awning is. Look at this roof. It could cave any minute. When we were here Friday night, wasn't it, I don't know, cheerier?"

"It was dark when we were here, but the lights on the place made it look cozy, yes. Welcoming."

John looked out at the few light posts dotting the perimeter of the small parking lot.

Ivy followed his gaze before a smear of motion in her peripheral vision snapped her attention back to the window he'd been trying to peer through. *I'm sure nothing's watching us from an abandoned building.*

"Yeah, we definitely need Adam to come up with some theories on this," John said. "Each one of those lights has a missing or broken bulb. What are the chances of that?"

She returned to following his gaze, assessing the three lamp posts, which she could have sworn were ornamental, wrought iron Friday night. Today they were typical, standard-issue, low-bid contractor's lights. Just missing the bulbs. "Considering the place looks like it was abandoned during the Great Depression, I think chances are good the bulbs would be missing and the parking lot would be full of potholes."

He shifted his gaze to the asphalt before them. "This place was safe and well-lined Friday night," he said.

"Agreed," she said.

"Yep. I'll ask Adam what causes a Christmas shop to suddenly decay."

"Again, I ask why a state university professor will have insight on...on whatever we think's happening here?"

"The guy has enough bizarre ideas to convince me he'd know *what* to research in this situation. I have no idea where to start when it comes to figuring out how to irritate or placate spirits in the woods. If Meghan Temple has disappeared—which is what I think has happened here—after selling a talisman to an unsuspecting teenager a few houses down from an architect who designs houses where the woods used to be, we might need Adam's unconventional research ideas."

Ivy shivered. "It might be convoluted, but you just made it sound somehow plausible. Realistic. As if Meghan really could've been selling crap that called forth angry spirits."

"Let's hope I'm just imagining crazy stuff," he said, motioning for her to proceed him back toward the SUV. "And let's get back to the house before someone decides to go looking for a tree without me along."

The tree situation wasn't going to resolve itself and became almost a debate topic as the two families finished an evening meal together. The girls had returned from school and the Stovalls from their offices and they all had different reasons for wanting or not wanting a tree in the house.

"We'll avoid lights, of course," Candy said. "But I think the tradition of setting up the tree will be healthy. And making it a group activity should be therapeutic. Don't you think?"

John acquiesced to taking Harry to pick out a tree for the two families to decorate together, but only if the remaining family members all promised to stay indoors and together while the two were away. Lexie wanted to go along. John and her parents vetoed her participation. No amount of whining from Lexie could persuade John to change his mind, and he finally sat her down in the great room and locked her in a serious gaze.

"Lexie, do you know what tools they use at Christmas tree farms?" he asked.

The question startled the girl because she'd immediately understood the answer. "Oh my God. Chainsaws. It'll sound like chainsaws there." The hint of hysteria entering her voice set even Ivy on edge.

John put a hand on the girl's shoulder to ground her. "While they're very safe, they will be noisy. You don't need to be there."

Lexie agreed.

John and Harry left without further argument from anyone.

But once the two were away, Adam groused about it. "They could get an artificial tree without any trauma for anyone. The tree included."

Ivy sat down on one of the couches with her laptop and grinned at the fellow who reminded her of an eighties private eye. "Only trauma for the sweatshop workers in the plastics factories."

Adam frowned at her. "Not all artificial trees are made of plastic."

"That's true. Some have even higher carbon footprints and price tags. Do you know how many years you have to keep an artificial tree in your home before its carbon footprint is finally offset by growing one real Christmas tree on a farm?"

"You're going to be a very difficult person to spend the holidays with," Adam said.

She shrugged. "Hopefully not. I'm teasing you to see if you'll add artificial trees to your research over there."

The man *harrumphed* as he returned to his own laptop. She assumed he looked up information about silver and its conductivity for supernatural forces after secret stores closed down. John had had a lengthy conversation with the man upon their return from the disappointing Mistletoe excursion, after all. She and John had both hoped the good professor would say something miraculous and resolute like, "Ah, with the store condemned and the shopkeeper gone, the talisman will be devoid of power."

That was far from Adam's assessment.

While John had discussed paranormal activities with the good professor, Ivy had managed to mangle one of the doctor's transcriptions she'd set as a goal to complete that day. She hoped to get it re-edited before John and Harry returned with the Christmas tree, but the polite bickering between Candy and Arthur spilling into the great room became distracting.

"He suggested we should do normal things to settle our nerves," Candy was saying.

She spoke of the police officer, Ben Riley. Ivy had decided the officer reminded her of the sheriff in the movie *Signs*, suggesting the family do normal things to get their minds off a tragic death. *He should've suggested we go to town and eat a pizza.*

"Watching cartoons isn't something we normally do," Arthur argued.

"No, but watching *A Charlie Brown Christmas* is tradition," Candy said.

"I vote for the Charlie Brown thing," Lizzy called from the couch where she lounged next to her moody sister.

Now that she listened to Arthur and Candy bickering, Ivy felt a twinge of regret for needling the professor. Especially for doing so in front of Lexie and Lizzy. They didn't need to see adults jabbing each other.

Arthur was polite enough not to argue directly with the child who had lost her home. He put on a fake smile and addressed the girl with, "Then Charlie Brown it will be. I'm sure there's popcorn in the pantry that Candy can fix for you if you all want to assemble in the theatre upstairs."

Ah, that's his way of getting rid of all of us.

She wondered if he had an evening of heavy sexting planned. Was that his new normal?

Chapter 22

Candy spoke: "We can't sit around dreading the moment one of Arthur's enemies will show up demanding his head on a platter." It was Wednesday afternoon and she'd coaxed Ivy, Harry, and Adam to the movie room upstairs with wine where she fiddled with electronic equipment.

"That's nice," Harry sauced. "Maybe a little Christmas cheer could bring some *good* luck to us?"

Candy grinned at her son. "I have Christmas cheer. I also have no more patience with the negativity happening around Reindeer Creek this season. We're gonna make our own good juju."

"Starting with electronic entertainment in the middle of the afternoon?" her son asked.

"Yes. Starting with electronic entertainment in the middle of the afternoon."

"Projecting video games on a movie screen seems a bit juvenile," Adam suggested. "Perhaps we could take turns reading from Dickens. *A Christmas Carol* would be an ideal work to put us in a festive—"

Candy pointed at him. "*You* need more to drink."

"Mom."

Candy stuck her tongue between her teeth to grimace at them.

Ivy chuckled at the men in the room. "All right. Let's give our hostess a break. She's been through a lot the past couple of weeks. If she wants to set up a competition for destroying elves or whatever she's got going on there to spread wacky joy for a little while, I say let's join in. I'm game. Harry? Are you game?"

Harry shook his head slightly. "Yeah, I'm in." He looked to his professor in the seat beside him. "I apologize for whatever this is gonna be."

"Hey now. There are no apologies for your mom's madness," Candy said.

"Oh, wait. Is this gonna be TikToks?" Harry asked. "I know you like to share TikToks you find."

"There *should* be apologies for TikToks," Adam muttered.

"I agree with you there," Ivy said lowly. She leaned toward Adam in the fancy theatre seats and spoke conspiratorially. "Candy gets tickled by a few specific accounts and shares the links with me. Some can be very entertaining, if vapid."

"They require inebriation," Harry said.

"You shouldn't know such a thing," Ivy said. "And you shouldn't be on, what is that? Your third glass? You can't show up to a Christmas party tonight inebriated. You're underage."

"He's certainly *not* going to Carole Marrack's house if he's inebriated," Candy said.

"I think I'll need a third glass if we're about to watch Christmas Toks," the lad said.

"It's like listening to Britney Spears singing 'My Only Wish' in every store you enter this time of year," Adam groused. "Complete with the drum machine brought to the forefront."

"Hey now, that's getting awfully close to denigrating Mariah Carey's 'All I Want for Christmas' song," Ivy warned.

"And would that be so wrong?" Adam asked.

"I don't know why, but I love that ridiculous thing," Ivy admitted.

"The Mariah Carey song?" Adam asked, fully aghast.

"Yep. I don't know what's wrong with me, but I love it. No lie: I sing along in the truck."

Harry laughed out loud. "Probably not since it was playing when that wolf attacked us Friday night. But *this* I've gotta hear. Aunt Ivy singing along with a poppy Christmas diva."

Adam smiled with half his mouth. He set his wine glass in the holder built into the armrest as if tapping a gavel gently against a sound block. "I would also find this amusing."

Candy clapped her hands rapidly with joy. "I almost have the karaoke machine set up! We can totally do this!"

"We totally can't," Ivy responded.

"Is that what you're doing?" Harry asked.

"I find it difficult to believe she's setting up a karaoke machine with the amount of wine she's imbibed this afternoon," Adam droned.

"Hey," Candy said. "I've had one glass. One. I've been playing hostess and getting things set up to entertain you all. And I think this is ready. So, what'll it be? 'All I Want for Christmas Is You?' Is that the first one?"

"Please. I'd pay money to hear Aunt Ivy sing it," Harry said.

"I'd pay money to get *out* of singing it," Ivy said.

"Oooo, you guys could do 'Baby, It's Cold Outside,' together," Candy giggled merrily.

Ivy rolled her eyes.

"No," Adam stated succinctly.

"Mom," Harry warned. "Seriously."

"If you're going to retain my interest, I will require one more glass of wine and something less assault-y," Ivy said.

"Yeah, yeah, yeah, I hear ya," Candy said, scrolling through the Tablet before her. "Here we go. How about Wham!'s 'Last Christmas?' That should be right up your alley, Miss Ivy. Very eighties and Christmas poppy."

"I acquiesce," Ivy said.

Candy grinned at her. "To the stage with you both."

"I don't believe that song is a duet," Adam said.

Ivy spoke to him in conspiratorial tones now. "It's not, but we're not getting out of this unscathed. Sing and get it over with."

He nodded and followed her—as if being led to the gallows—to the side of the machine's monitor. They woodenly accepted microphones from Candy.

"Does she keep this set up here all year?" Adam asked.

Ivy smiled at him, pleased to tease her friend. "You'd think so, right? But I think this is for impromptu holiday entertaining. Or randomly embarrassing her guests."

"The words aren't coming up," Candy groused. "Why aren't the words coming up?"

"I don't need the words," Ivy said.

Adam gasped. "You're telling me you've got this song memorized?"

"Do not question Aunt Ivy's knowledge of eighties lyrics," Harry said.

"It's from nineteen eighty-five," Ivy said to Adam.

"Yes, but that doesn't mean everyone knows all the words," he explained.

"Dude, you're at least the same age I am. We've both been hearing this song every Christmas since nineteen eighty-five. How do you not know all the words?"

"Dude," he muttered. "I'm not a dude."

"That's the truth," she muttered back.

"I know the words," John said in his amused baritone. Ivy and Adam looked to the back of the room where the bodyguard had quietly stepped into the scene. As he was wont to do.

"Oh, here we go!" Candy announced happily. "I got it. Words. Here we go. Are you two ready?" She beamed at the two who were no longer looking at each other. As if purposely ignoring the tension between the frowning singers next to her, Candy said, "I'm hitting the button. Get ready."

"If he knows the words, let him make a fool of himself instead," Adam said, holding the microphone out toward the advancing bodyguard.

Harry grinned at his blushing "Aunt Ivy," and said, "I'd pay to see them sing this as a duet."

Before John reached the front of the theatre, Lexie appeared in the doorway, breathless and anxious. "You guys! That tree guy is back! The one that died!"

Chapter 23

Adam Thackery hesitated while the other adults in the theatre rushed to follow the suddenly appearing teenager hobble-clomping down the staircase. He wasn't a fearful man. He'd come up against his share of supernatural entities during the random séance or witching hour.

It wasn't something a person brought up in polite society.

But it was something a person alluded to when kids absently used talismans to summon winter beasts to kill innocent landscapers. Or whatever was going on around this neighborhood. He'd suggested to the security man, John Knightley, that the teenager with the necklace was channeling spirits she knew nothing about. Mr. Knightley had been appropriately skeptical. And then the man had started putting all the puzzle pieces together and had come to Adam for additional research.

Adam didn't need to do additional research to tell these people they had a spirit from the neighboring property trying to protect itself against further encroachment. These people were lucky it hadn't burned down all their homes and killed every last one of them for the wasteful houses already erected here.

He wondered what on Earth he could do to help the poor child who'd brought it all upon them.

*****

Dash Heggs, the recently dead, stood on the front porch of the Harris house. With his right arm across his eviscerated lower torso, he held his intestines within his roundness. He kept internal organs behind splintered rib bones with his left arm across his chest.

Surprisingly, nothing dripped from the meat-packed smell on the front porch. No chunks of flesh fell off dangling sinew. It was as if his condition was frozen in place in a newly failed meat locker. Like a candle's wax after the flame's been extinguished.

Lexie trembled as she peered around Ivy's arm.

"What the actual hell?" John asked. "Is this—is this real? What am I looking at?"

"I've come to warn you," Dash said. His mouth moved, but not in sync with the words. The sound was at least one beat ahead of the lips' movement and another beat ahead of a flatulence that reeked of perforated bowels.

Harry put an arm in front of his mother, as if they were in a fast-moving car and Candy was without a seatbelt. John took one step forward onto the threshold to represent the small group.

"What do you want to warn us about?"

"You're not supposed to talk to ghosts," Lexie whispered.

Dash's eyes shifted, the painted plaster color fixing on the girl. The girl who carried the silver circle. "I've come to warn you that you carry the talisman. The spirit of the sacred land knows you have it. The spirit of the sacred land will move through it and destroy those who desecrate the sacred land."

Ivy had a pretty good idea of what the talisman was at this point. She could guess the sacred land was the property behind them, but she wanted to be sure. If they were dealing with real, honest-to-goodness paranormal entities, then by God she wanted to be sure.

"Where is the sacred land?" she asked.

"You stand on sacred land."

Candy gasped.

With a moan that started somewhere in his lower intestines, Dash began to groan. Ivy frowned at what looked like swelling in the dead man's hands and wrists.

"Is he expanding?" Harry asked in disbelief.

"Time to get inside," John announced, backing into the house. He pushed the four of them out of the way as he slammed the door against a ripping, splattering squelch of bone and flesh exploding against the house.

"I'm gonna be sick," Candy said.

"No. No, you're gonna help me make a plan," Ivy said. "This stops today. That thing was a zombie, right?"

"Or a ghost," Lexie said.

"So, it was giving us a warning from the other side," Ivy said. *Funny how one ghost's appearance can make you a believer.*

John paced in front of the door, running his hand through his hair.

"It was telling us some kind of spirit is mad about these houses being on this land, right?" Ivy continued.

"Are we supposed to pack up and leave?" Harry asked. "We can't do anything about these houses being here."

"Is that why my house burned down?" Lexie asked.

Ivy wasn't stopping to answer questions. She had a goal. "We have to let the spirit know that it's not your fault that these houses are here. We have to let it know Arthur is trying to stop anyone from stealing the rest of the land over there." She pointed toward the back of the house. "To build more crap on."

John stopped pacing to face her. "How do we communicate with a spirit? Its spokesperson just exploded on the front porch."

"Wait a minute," Candy said. "We're gonna believe there's a spirit that hates us being here? What makes us think that's real?"

Lexie pointed toward the door. "There's dead-guy guts all over your front porch."

"There's a spiritual war going on around us every day," Ivy said. "I mean, that's the sort of thing you think of happening within The Church or being handled by priests and exorcists, not random people out here, right? But demons and bad things really do target your everyday human. Spiritual warfare really does happen on the layperson level. We don't see it, but it's there. With this talisman introduced to our lives, we're being shown how real it is."

"What's this talisman?" Candy asked.

"Oh, yeah, you haven't been in on that conversation," Lexie said. She pulled the necklace from under her shirt so Candy could see the silver pendant. "This handle from the silver bells is part of it. I think I broke the talisman so it's in two parts."

"And I think we can solve two problems with one broken talisman," Ivy said.

Chapter 24

Wednesday night's party arrived sooner than any of them wanted. Ivy rushed around her room getting ready mere minutes before they were to leave. She had the cocktail dress on her body but that was about as ready as she felt when someone knocked on her door. *Oh, thank goodness. Candy can zip this thing up for me.*

She dropped her hairbrush on the end of the bed as she rushed to the door, and, as she lifted her hair off her back and spun, called, "Come in, come in and zip this for me, sweetie."

The door opened.

She continued telling Candy, "I called to let Carole know we were bringing cookies but didn't have time to make dip, and she sounded very put out about it. She's a little high-strung, isn't she?"

The hands at the small of her back were not Candy's but they moved the zipper up to the center of her back smoothly. "I had to act in a play directed by Carole Marrack not a week ago," John Knightley admitted.

She spun again, this time releasing her hair, and stared at him in shock. "Oh my God. I'm so sorry."

He smirked. "You look incredible. Candy is beside herself because we're going to be late arriving at this woman's house with only cookies. So, I'm here to see if there's anything you need."

Anything I need?

"Of course, I told her I'd be useless helping you get ready for a Christmas party. But that turned out to be wrong."

"I'm—I thought Candy had come up—"

"As I surmised."

Gawd. There's that dead-sexy smile. What a shame we have to fight evil tonight. It'd be so much nicer to hang out together at the party and maybe slow dance.

"Ivy?"

"Hmm?"

"I asked if you needed me to carry anything down to the car? You know. Paranormal fighting weaponry suggested by our good professor. That sort of thing."

She laughed lightly. "Ah, yes. Silver bullets? Maybe wooden stakes and a crossbow to fire them from? I don't think we get to follow the usual monster-fighting tropes for this one." She grabbed her handbag from the foot of the bed and checked inside. "Just a cell phone and silver talisman with some ribbon and mistletoe." She looked back up at him leaning against the doorframe.

Gentleman's not stepping into my room uninvited? God bless, this guy's too good to be true.

"Those will have to do for our non-Hollywood hijinks," she said.

He smiled. "I have some old standards on standby. Let's go."

*****

Professor Adam Thackery assured the two families he'd join them shortly and waved from the pool of golden light as they drove away. He closed the front door and turned to lean his back against it. Candy had walked him through how to set the alarm so he could leave the house safe and sound after his evening meditation. Given what he knew of John Knightley's plan to court an offended spirit tonight, he wished to set the alarm immediately and huddle in the kitchen.

While setting the alarm would cause problems if he forgot about it and opened any doors later, he intended to enact the second half of the plan. Hide in the pantry.

Yes, these were the misgivings of a coward. But this coward understood the supernatural. And intended to remain cautious.

If he'd learned anything in his forty years of teaching metaphysics, he knew the quartet of John Knightley, Ivy Light, Lexie Stovall, and Michael "Harry" Harris drew the demons and dangers of the neighboring woods to one location tonight—luckily it wasn't the house where Adam now switched off the overhead chandelier lighting. The offended spirit of the Reindeer Creek woods and prairie would believe no one remained behind. This would be the safest mansion on Chestnut Parkway tonight.

Or so Adam repeated to himself as he tip-toed across the graying foyer under the watchful gaze of the silent wolf on the landing.

Chapter 25

C arole Marrack resembled a white's tree frog in both facial expression and attitude. For a wealthy woman hosting the most decadent party of the holiday season, she should have been swirling through her multi-million-dollar mansion with nothing but smiles and bright, shining eyes. Instead, she pursed her lips as if the last fly she ate had been sprayed with Raid. She needed to go spit it out.

She looked at Ivy as if examining all her flaws. "Interesting. You're Candace Harris' houseguest? You're the one who called with her excuses about not bringing a simple side dish to a party she had months to prepare for."

Ivy performed a mock curtsy and said, "For which she had months to prepare."

John stifled his laugh behind a cough and moved away from the women.

"I beg your pardon?" Carole said.

"Is there a coat room?" Ivy asked. "Or will we be required to carry our winter coats throughout the evening?"

The tree frog woman hitched one side of her mouth upward. "Charming." She raised a hand and snapped her fingers at a man in a tuxedo. "Daniel.

The Harris party has arrived and needs to be shown to the cloak room."

Lexie put her arm through Ivy's to tag along and a swirl of peppermint wafted from the girl's purse to Ivy. "Oh my God. That was bad-ass. Did you correct her grammar?"

"Yeah, it probably wasn't the politest thing I've done today, but she made me fussy. Don't follow my example, okay?"

Lexie giggled. "In this crazy flippin' holiday, it's nice to have something to laugh at once in a while."

"Like the quartet she has playing in the foyer?" Ivy asked.

Lexie giggled again, but Ivy glanced over her shoulder at the cello player struggling to bow his instrument while disinterested partygoers walked within his personal space. Carole Marrack should've erected rope and stanchion in front of the quartet to keep people from tripping into the music stands.

Things could get ridiculous in this part of the house if people knocked over the musicians.

With their coats deposited in the cloak room and Candy's Tupperware containers emptied onto Mikasa bell-shaped platters, the women divided up to make their way into the throng.

"The McGwires canceled today," someone said as Ivy passed a group of heavy jasmine.

"The Sheppards canceled today," someone said as she passed another group, this one heavy with cinnamon and anise.

With Candy distracted by a neighbor, Ivy caught Marna Stovall's attention. "Are there prominent families missing from the party or something?"

The woman nodded, fanning herself with a lacy handkerchief. "I learned at work today that several people who'd RSVP'd backed out. One of the commissioners decided it would be poor form to attend a party next door to a tragedy. And in light of Raya Kelter's death over the weekend. She was chosen as the soloist not for her voice, you know."

They'd moved into a room where a long table of petit fours and miniature pies sat about three feet from a wall of framed mirrors. The chamber music from the foyer couldn't possibly cut into this low din of voices so a deejay perched in the corner playing Susan Boyle's "Hark the Herald Angels Sing."

One less commissioner available to locate. Darn. Aloud, Ivy asked, "Raya Kelter wasn't the first choice?"

"Oh, she was the first choice. She was the only choice. Her godfather is Dayton Manti." Marna nodded toward a trim older man in the expected tuxedo on the far side of the room, near the exit to a patio full of lights and pouting patio heaters.

Ivy played the name in her brain, running it through a catalog of conversations. She was pretty sure Candy had mentioned this man in the past. Perhaps six months ago. Or while sifting through ash and soot. The name had a dirty feel to it.

"He never married so he has all his money."

Ivy looked to Marna's wistful countenance. The woman had grabbed a martini off a tray circulating the crowd and now winked at Ivy over the lip of the glass. After sipping, she repeated herself. "All of his money. This means families are happy to name him godfather for their kids."

"Interesting," Ivy said.

"Well. Except Arthur and Candy. They didn't. I don't know if Arthur knew Dayton back when Michael was born. Michael. Harry. It's hard to remember to call him Harry, isn't it? I've only known him a year, but, you know what I mean."

"Mmm. I've known him all his life so, yes, I know what you mean."

"But Dayton would make a great godfather at any point in life. The man's loaded. And has influence. He could help Arthur get out of whatever trouble he's in with the unions. He's connected."

Ivy pretended this wasn't alarming for Marna to say out loud.

"Ladies," Harry said, sidling up to them. "I've lost track of everyone already. This house is huge."

Marna smiled before returning to her martini and walking cautiously toward the refreshment tables.

"It would be good to keep track of Lexie," Ivy said.

He nodded. "Understood. I'll find her in just one minute. Let me say 'hey' to these fellas."

He stepped over to a group that joyfully pulled him in with, "Michael! How's college life treatin' ya?"

"Great, great. I invited one of my professors to this shindig but haven't seen him yet."

"Schmoozing the professors. Good for you," one of the men said.

Another man furrowed his brow at Harry. "Didn't I just see you in a different jacket?"

Harry shook his head with a grin. "Nope. I've been wearing this all evening. Tell me about your twins, man. How's married life for you?"

Ivy looked away from that group to see what Dayton Manti was up to. Surprisingly, Arthur had joined him at the high-top table and the two seemed engrossed in conversation.

Surely, this isn't going to be that easy.

Chapter 26

The plan had been to look for a commissioner—or two—and corner them. But this might turn out just as good. She plucked a glass of something icy with a straw in it from a passing waiter's tray and stepped close enough to the table to hear them clearly over the soft and sweet tones of Susan Boyle singing, "it's that time of year when the world falls in love." She kept her back to them in hopes they wouldn't figure out she was eavesdropping, swaying slightly to the Christmas waltz.

"You're telling me you knew the service?" Arthur was asking.

"Come on, man. It wasn't a real tree service," Dayton scoffed. "Heggs was there to get some information for me, maybe scare you into finally coming to your senses. I don't know how you did it, but murdering the man on your own property? That took balls. I didn't think you had that kind of fortitude."

In the mirrors across the room, Ivy watched Arthur hold up his drink as if in a salute to the man. As if he'd had anything to do with the gruesome death of a lawn-ornament-come-to-life in his backyard. What Ivy couldn't understand was why Dayton Manti thought Mr. Heggs was a real person. She wondered if John needed to do a search for the real-world Dash Heggs and make sure the guy was all right.

Alive and all that.

"I tell you what," Dayton said. "That property behind your house is huge. Expansive. It can be parceled up. Let's say we make a deal, you and me. You know as well as I do the commissioners want the taxes it'll generate. You're not gonna win that fight. But we could strike a balance."

"Maybe you didn't catch on the past six months after all," Arthur said.

Ivy pretended to suck on the straw between her lips. She pretended she wasn't smiling at Arthur standing up for one of the few good things about himself. She pretended she wasn't listening to the conversation taking place at the high-top table behind her.

"No, now, hear me out," Dayton argued like a seasoned politician. Or peddler of souls. The two were often difficult to differentiate. "Because I've got a deal for you. You don't want to hire from the union. You don't want us turning that property into low-income housing and strip malls. How about we divide that property back there into two sections? One that remains protected and pristine up against the Reindeer Creek subdivision you and your neighbors are so proud of and one that my godson gets to develop into whatever the commissioners ask him to develop with union workers who never bother you again."

Arthur frowned. "You're asking me to stop fighting an illegal land-grab to get bullies to stop harassing me and my family into union contracts?"

The man smiled patiently. "Yes."

Susan started singing "in the bleak midwinter" overhead and Ivy thought the timing fitting. *The deejay's playing her whole Christmas album.*

"Who's this godson you want to bestow so much illegal activity on?" Arthur asked.

"Ah, yes. You really should meet this fellow." Dayton turned toward the refreshments table and scanned the crowd. He spied Harry and raised his hand as if to wave. Then stopped. "Oh, my goodness. Wrong lad."

In her mind, Ivy remembered John's voice on the phone saying, "He's the spitting image of Michael Harris."

Oh my God. Meghan's son is here. He brought Meghan's son to confront Arthur.

Dayton signaled to a man seated in the shadows beyond the table, and as that person rose, he turned back to Arthur. "They look so much alike."

Ivy turned around and set her glass heavily on the high-top table between them. "Gentlemen, my apologies. Arthur, I think you need to get out of here."

"Excuse me?" Dayton practically sputtered. "Who are you?"

"I'm the gal who's about to summon hell on Earth. I think." She pulled the silver bells from her purse and slammed it on the table with what she hoped was a commanding force.

"Arthur Harris has been trying to protect his family and the sacred land behind the property he did not desecrate," she announced.

The man who'd risen to approach them stopped walking. Unfortunately, he stopped next to Harry and people gasping at the resemblance distracted her for a second.

Focus.

"Arthur's tried to protect the land he's not responsible for desecrating," she repeated. "It's not his fault or his family's fault that the land was rezoned or deforested. That sin is the fault of people like you, Dayton Manti. Arthur has been trying to stop you and your county commissioners from doing more harm these past six months. You." She pointed at him as she took one step back from the table. "And your partners are responsible for the building taking place on sacred land. You and your partners are responsible for the man who tried to cut down trees on sacred land this week. You are responsible."

"What's wrong with you?" Dayton interrupted. "Who are you?"

From beside Harry, Lexie nervously rubbed the pendant at her neck. "Oh, man. I think he's in a lot of trouble."

No one else in the room moved or spoke for a moment. The music overhead ceased as the deejay stopped the CD. From the hall, stringed instruments softly filtered through tinkling glasses and jovial voices until a woman's scream shattered it all.

"There it is," Ivy said.

Arthur glanced out the doors to his right where the patio heaters guttered away but people stopped their merrymaking to look inside.

Dayton Manti reached out to grab Ivy's arm. "There what is? Who are you?"

"I'm an outsider, looking in at the war you started."

A gentleman in combat boots strode in from Arthur's right and fixed Manti in a glare. "Hands off the lady." Because he spoke with authority, like a mercenary or freedom fighter, Dayton obeyed. The man came around the table and behind Ivy, putting his hands to her upper arms as if he hadn't just ordered someone else against that very thing.

He glared at Arthur. "You're Arthur Harris?"

"Yes."

"You. Take Ivy." He pressed Ivy toward him. "Hide."

"Wait. Who are you?" Ivy asked.

"Jack Henry. I work for John. He's getting Candace out of danger, but this is about to get messy."

"Messy?" Arthur questioned.

Jack gave Ivy a look that suggested things were already messy, but she didn't understand. *How does this guy know what's going on here?*

"You should be moving toward a hiding place," he said.

But it was too late for hiding.

Chapter 27

ohn had been standing outside the parlor where Ivy listened to Arthur's conversation with Union Boss Dayton Manti. He'd completed a circuit of the perimeter and discovered Jack doing the same. "Good to see you here for our big night," he joked.

"Don't like the sound of that," Jack said.

"We've got this idea that we can direct a demon toward the bad guys. You down with that?"

Jack started to laugh, then sobered up. "Christ, you're being serious. Is that why there's a dead guy in the Harris' kitchen?"

"Dead guy?" John startled. "Who's still at the— oh man. Professor Thackery."

"The kid's professor?"

"I bet," John guessed. "He was supposed to join us here tonight."

"The kid's not getting that A after all," Jack said.

"Right. Okay. Down to it. My client's family and the family they took in after the fire are both in this house, scattered. Thackery helped Ivy and me come up with a plan to draw out this thing that's been stalking them and turn it on the county commissioners who've been threatening my client. It's weird. It's not something you can digest in one sitting like this. But it's gonna get—"

"What?" Jack asked when his boss stared into the distance instead of talking. "Messy?"

"I think it's here. Look at this."

Jack followed John's nod toward mist and fog swarming over the posh in-ground pool behind them.

"Whoa. That's not natural," Jack said.

"That's not the half of it," John muttered. "Can you keep track of Ivy in here?"

"Yes, if you—"

"I'm getting Candy and the girls out of the kitchen. One of the girls is wearing a talisman that'll attract this thing."

"Okay, but—"

"Kill anything that looks other-worldly before it can kill you," John said.

And with that strange order, John ran around the front of the house. Jack assumed he knew the quickest way to the kitchen where a girl with a talisman endangered one of his clients. It was the strangest debriefing he'd ever been through. And it didn't prepare him for people to start screaming and throwing Christmas wreaths and garland around to escape wolf-like creatures leaping across the pool and patio and up the side of the mansion.

He ran ahead of them into the parlor and slammed the French doors behind him, yelling at a mafia-looking businessman gripping the person he was pretty sure John had pointed to when referencing "Ivy."

*****

Something more than wolves crashed into the parlor as Arthur pulled Ivy toward a bank of potted Christmas trees.

"Wait. No. Let me go," she fussed, yanking her arm from Arthur's grip. "Lexie."

"Whatever," Arthur said, practically diving behind the row of trees.

The mayhem in the parlor matched what took place in other rooms of the giant house. Gray mist and black wolves swirled and loped through the halls seeking their prey, and people screamed running from the nightmare.

As Ivy pulled her arm from Arthur, she bumped directly into Dayton Manti. He stood as a wall of anger and barked in her face, "Tell me what's going on here."

"They're coming for you. Out of my way."

"Who's coming for me? Who are you?"

"I told you, I'm—"

This was all they had time for before being interrupted by the blast of a gun in their near vicinity. It rang in their ears, making it difficult to hear anything else.

While a great deal of breaking and smashing of pedestals and expensive crystal took place as adults ran in frantic panic, the destruction was short-lived in their immediate room. Harry had pulled Lexie under a dessert table to hide her from danger. He popped back up to help Ivy but found himself face to face with some kind of gray bear-like creature with crooked teeth reaching for him. "Whoa!"

Jack Henry strode forward, leveled a handgun at the side of the thing's head, and squeezed the trigger. Gray and red splatter exploded toward the doorway and the creature dropped in a heap of mottled fur.

"Thanks," Harry shouted.

"It looked other-worldly to me," Jack said, not trying to accommodate the ringing in anyone's ears.

"Whatever, man. Thanks," Harry yelled over the sudden deafness of being so close to a fired weapon.

He spun to the table behind him and scanned for a weapon. He grabbed a fork-looking utensil. He had no clue what the elite called the thing, but it looked pointy enough to pierce skin if he put some force behind the thrust.

"Here," Lexie called up to him. She held out a metal kitchen tool—a meat tenderizer clumped with what looked and smelled like peppermint candy bits. While his brain told him this made no sense at all, he thanked his stars for the solidity of the hammer and its spiky top. He grabbed it from her and turned back to the room.

Recovering from the gunshot so near at hand, Dayton grabbed the silver bells from the high-top table to his left and shook it at Ivy. "What is this?"

She took a step away from him, which should have been his red flag moment.

He shouted the question again, but his answer came in the form of a huge black wolf crashing through the glass window beside the high-top table. It leapt through glass and sheer curtains and wooden table to knock Dayton further into the room a good three or four steps.

He ducked, using his arms to shield his face from the splintering, shattering wood and glass, and when he stood upright again, the monster stood where the table had once been. It glowered at the pair staring at it in shock.

Until Ivy moved.

She pointed at the man beside her and shouted above the ringing in her ears, above the screaming in the room, above the yelling that sounded like her name. "He's the one you want!"

"What? No!"

The wolf didn't waste another breath but leapt onto the man holding the silver bells. It clamped its jaws around Dayton's throat and shook as the two landed on the fine, expensive carpet of Carole Marrack's fine, expensive house.

Its front claws against Dayton's chest already pierced the jacket, vest, silk shirt, skin, and muscle on the way down, and the impact with the floor helped drive nails between rib bone and into precious organs. With ancient hate, the wolf raked its claws outward and downward toward the floor, ripping the dying man's chest in eight shredding, bleeding strips. With his vocal cords flying in mini chunks to the left and right of his head, Dayton couldn't scream.

I've got to move. I've got to get away from this.

Ivy looked past the feasting wolf to the table where Harry stood in shock with a pair of kitchen utensils held up by his face. Under the table, Lexie sobbed into her arms folded over her knees.

Jack popped back into the room. "The hall's clear. Let's go—whoa." He pointed the gun at the wolf devouring Dayton on the floor, but the sloppy beast wasn't looking up yet.

Ivy put one finger to her lips and motioned for the others to come to her. She turned to the French doors and opened them to the cold night and a towering wolf standing on its back legs. It stared down at her with a growl that she imagined she heard.

Oh no.

"Here, here, wait, no, give it this, wait, wait," Lexie stammered, crawling out from under the table. She struggled to crawl in her long skirt while pulling the silver pendant out from under the front of her dress.

"Oh, Lexie, stay back," Ivy begged.

The wolf between them lifted its head from its meal and locked its eyes on Lexie's hand where the silver circle swung.

The girl struggled again getting the chain around her head, mussing and pulling her hair as she tugged it free. She held it out in front of her as she walked slowly forward. Harry matched her gait, staying at her side.

"This is messed up," Jack muttered to himself. He kept the gun trained on the wolf inside the room, the one now sitting on its haunches, dripping blood from its messy jaws.

Then Ivy heard John's voice. She couldn't be sure—given the damage from the recent gunfire—whether he was in the room or in a tunnel far away, but she heard him say, "On three."

Jack reacted to this by saying, "One."

John's voice said, "Two."

Chapter 28

The explosion of gunfire deafened Ivy again but she had the presence of mind to step aside as the head of the tall wolf before her exploded and the creature fell in a heap at her feet. John stepped past it, kicking it to the side, and reached for her. She took his hand and he pulled her to his chest. The rumble of him barking orders to the others shook against her but she couldn't hear his voice yet. Her ears hurt with the ringing.

She looked back to see Lexie crumpled against Harry, who swung an honest-to-God meat tenderizer into the eye socket of a leaping wolf. The beast dropped like a sack of bricks before them, thus before Harry's doppelganger, who stared wide-eyed with mouth agape. The man was obviously as frightened by what took place here as any other reasonable person would be.

None of us are going to be reasonable for a while.

As John pulled her toward the doors of the patio, she glanced to Dayton's body where the other wolf now lay dead, draped across the man he'd killed. She couldn't see the silver bells statue that had started this mess.

John peeled off his jacket and placed it on a cold concrete bench next to the pool. Then he sat her on one portion of the jacket and Lexie immediately next to her. As if she wouldn't naturally do this, he lifted one of her arms around Lexie's shoulders. She watched him in the sparkly light of Lalique crystal bulbs hung in mockery of their distress.

He pointed toward the house, motioning in a sweeping gesture, obviously offering orders to the man named Jack Henry. Jack nodded and jogged in that direction. Pulling an earplug from his left ear, John offered an order to Harry next; and the lad went back into the parlor, still carrying the murderous kitchen utensils.

Then John turned to her. He typed on his cell phone as he walked toward her. He held the phone up where she could see the screen. It read: "I know you can't hear from all the gunfire."

She half laughed at this, and he pulled the phone back to his personal space to type again. This time, while typing, he stopped to speak to someone off to her right. When he finished, he held the phone out for her to read again.

"Candy, Lizzy, Marna = safe. Police are on the way. When house is clear, I'll get you in where it's warm."

She nodded at the message and said quietly, "If you held me, it would be warm."

She thought she could hear herself—thought the sounds of the words made sense in her own head. And when he smiled at her in the pretty light of a deathly Christmas party, she realized, he could hear her just fine. She blushed and tightened her grip on Lexie, who began to shake violently in her arms.

Because Ivy couldn't hear the footfalls of the rushing beast, she didn't know what frightened the girl in her arms. But she saw John react to something.

He pulled the gun from his hip holster and spun on his heel as a flurry of fur and darkness leapt in an almost graceful arc over a neighboring bench and into Harry's doppelganger. John fired into the beast, but Ivy certainly couldn't tell if he hit the thing as it ploughed into the young man. Both man and beast plunged into the heavy pool covering behind her. The tarp folded in on itself as water collapsed the edge of it, tangling wolf and strangling man in an icy deathtrap.

Ivy thought she heard a shout this time. She could swear she heard someone screaming John's name, screaming, "Don't you dare!" as she tugged at him, pulling him away from the edge of the pool, dragging him away from trying to jump into the frigid melee to save a man they didn't trust or believe was still alive. Her throat would be sore in the morning from trying to yell loud enough for the right words to be heard.

Chapter 29

Christmas morning dawned bright and shining with a glowing Christmas tree for both families. John Knightley sat back on one of the couches in the great room with Ivy Light in front of him, leaning on his chest as if they'd spent every Christmas morning this way. When he caught Jack Henry smirking at him, he merely smiled at the freelance employee. He could cancel Jack's next assignment if he gave him too much grief.

Lexie had just watched her mom opening a delicate box with a small crystal dove figurine. Marna smiled politely at her eldest daughter. "That's real sweet, Lexie. Thank you."

Lexie and Ivy exchanged a knowing look. Marna would never know what cursed present she almost received.

By the time special gifts of salvaged quilt scraps and precious knick-knacks mounted in a shadow box were open, the great room looked like a hurricane's aftermath of papers, tissue, boxes, ribbons, and even stray tape. The two families found themselves laughing about traditions and how they could get together for years into the future. The plan was for the Stovalls to move into a rental house in the school district while they rebuilt, rather than moving out of state with family far away, and they hoped to stay in touch with their new "family" here in Reindeer Creek.

When Candy went into the kitchen to get a trash bag for cleanup, Ivy grabbed a small box from beside her on the couch and followed. "I have something for you that I figured you'd want to open in private. Away from all the others."

As Candy spied the Under The Mistletoe giftbox, she snickered. "Is this proof that the spirits are appeased?"

"John and I think all the baddies took out their angst on the people who were responsible for this subdivision, yes."

Candy smiled. "Excellent. Then this also means the shopkeeper Meghan Temple is out of our lives?"

Ivy chuckled as she sat down at the island. "Now where did you hear that name?"

"Blast from the past," Candy said. "And back in the past."

"Good."

Ivy watched her friend lifting the top off the box and said, "You know he never met up with her, right?"

"I know," Candy said. "John told me it was all texting. All stuff online. And she started it and—oh my gosh. Ivy, this is lovely."

"I wanted to give you something for little Mindy," Ivy said. "I remember you saying her kicks were gentle like a dancer doing pirouettes. I wasn't sure if it would be appropriate after all, given everything that's happened the past couple of weeks."

"Oh, Ivy. This is beautiful," Candy breathed. "Thank you." She wrapped Ivy in a big bear hug. "I love it. Thank you."

As Ivy returned the hug, a pair of eyes watched through the kitchen window to the eerie chimes of silver bells on the air.

The End

Cast of Characters

While *Silver Bells* doesn't have a large cast to keep track of, here's a cheat sheet to help you monitor who's who. We'll start with our main character, Ivy Light. Then we have people listed in order of appearance with notation of importance to the story.

Ivy Light – Ivy is a forty-something gal who works as a medical transcriptionist/editor. She comes to her friend Candy Harris' home for an extended Christmas holiday out of a sense of obligation as well as love for her childhood friend. Ivy has zero romantic entanglements prior to our story, but she harbors a healthy appreciation for Jane Austen and British hotties with debonair features.
Story Importance: 10 Christmas Gnomes.

Lexie Stovall – Lexie is the sixteen-year-old girl who lost her house a couple of weeks before Christmas in a fire. She's not your typical surly teen but is figuring out how to roll with the crazy punches this Christmas is flinging at her.
Story Importance: 10 Christmas Gnomes.

Lizzy Stovall – Lizzy is the fourteen-year-old girl who lost her house a couple weeks before Christmas in a fire.
Story Importance: 4 Christmas Gnomes.

Leland and Marna Stovall – These are the aloof parents of Lexie and Lizzy. It's hinted they might have committed insurance fraud in the loss of their home, but this can't be proved. Due to the time of year, they don't rush right down to Louisiana to move in with family while a new house is built; instead, they accept the kind offer of neighbors Arthur and Candy Harris to use their basement apartment so the girls can stay in school, and Leland and Marna can continue their jobs "mostly uninterrupted" until after the first of the year.
Story Importance: 4 Christmas Gnomes for Marna; 3 for Leland.

Meghan Temple – Meghan Temple attended university with Ivy, Candy, and Arthur back in the day. She abruptly left school their freshman year, but has re-entered Arthur's life in the past six months.
Story Importance: 7.5 Christmas Gnomes.

John Knightley – John is the proprietor of Knightley Monitoring, a security service that employs bodyguards and escorts to protect private citizens. He's been personally guarding Arthur Harris since early July, and only recently sent two of his employees home for the holidays, thinking he could handle the entire Harris family on his own since they'll all be homebound for Christmas. He's the tall, dark, and handsome fellow who knows how to protect and serve without being overbearing.
Story Importance: 10 Christmas Gnomes.

The Reindeer Creek Spirit – In the woods and across the prairie of Reindeer Creek, an ancient and angry spirit wishes to reclaim its land. It manifests in a gray, wintery wind and in a pack of wolf-like creatures that obey its bidding.
Story Importance: 10 Christmas Gnomes.

Candace "Candy" Harris – Candy is the vivacious and kind-hearted housewife of the Harris household. She suffered a miscarriage about two years prior to our story and used much of the design of her new home as therapy. She's the endearing and lovely childhood friend that Ivy has come to the new neighborhood of Reindeer Creek to visit for the holidays, and she's done her level best to turn her home into a winter wonderland for the occasion without making her houseguests, who just lost their home to a Christmas-lights fire, uncomfortable.
Story Importance: 10 Christmas Gnomes.

Michael "Harry" Harris – Harry is the college son of Candy and Arthur. He's home for the holidays and has invited one of his professors to join his family as well. Story Importance: 7.5 Christmas Gnomes.

Arthur Harris – Arthur is a troubled businessman who has temptations and vexations assaulting him from all sides. He's not sure how to deal with any of it very well.
Story Importance: 5 Christmas Gnomes.

Raya Kelter – Poor Raya Kelter is a sixteen-year-old girl who was selected to sing a solo at the Christmas concert, not for her skill, but for her connection to the local business mogul, Mr. Dayton Manti.
Story Importance: 2.5 Christmas Gnomes.

Officer Ben Riley – The kind officer starts to recognize there's more going on at the Harris house than a few "dog" attacks and he wishes to help the kind and resourceful Ivy Light.
Story Importance: 2.5 Christmas Gnomes.

Mr. Klauss – The kind neighbor who lives across the street from the Harris family assisted Arthur in erecting the lights and décor so that it faced away from the woods because he knows things about the Reindeer Creek spirit.
Story Importance: 2.5 Christmas Gnomes.

Jack Henry – Jack is one of the freelance bodyguards John Knightley calls on from time to time. When John realizes the horrors stacking up around his client are more than he can handle on his own, he reaches out to Jack for last-minute Yuletide help—and Jack is the kind of reliable freelance muscle who responds.
Story Importance: 5 Christmas Gnomes.

Professor Adam Thackery – Adam is curmudgeonly at times, but a nice enough fellow. He understands more about talismans and offended spirits than does the family he's visiting.
Story Importance: 5 Christmas Gnomes.

Dash Heggs – Mr. Heggs is a landscaper whom we believe was "borrowed" by the Reindeer Creek spirit when Mr. Dayton Manti needed a lackey to do some dirty work.
Story Importance: 5 Christmas Gnomes.

Carole Marrack – This elegant socialite has nothing better to do with her time and wealth than coerce her neighbors into elaborate productions of plays and preparing competitive dishes for her black-tie parties.
Story Importance: 2.5 Christmas Gnomes.

Dayton Manti – Mr. Manti is a wealthy and well-connected union boss who wishes to exert much power and influence over Arthur.
Story Importance: 5 Christmas Gnomes.

**Other Holiday-Themed Stories
by Sandy Lender**
Dream Crystal for Christmas
(paranormal novella, 2020)

The *Faerie Holidays* Paranormal Satire Series
May Your Heart Be Light, book 1
My Faerie Valentine, book 2
I Know What Your Vampire Did Last Summer, book 3
Have Yourself a Faerie Little Christmas, book 4
(coming December 2024)

Also by Sandy Lender
The *Choices* Epic Fantasy Series
The *Dragons in Space* YA Sci-Fi/Fantasy Series
The *Faerie Holidays* Paranormal Satire Series
Poems of Trials, Triumphs, and Turtles
Poems of Fact, Form, and Fantasy
Destination Premeditation
Under the Ice
Return to the Tribe and Fire
*Move the Stars (*a *Gentle Dragons* novel*)*
How to Train Your Human: A Guide for Parrots
100 Things Duran Duran Fans
Should Know & Do During This Life

Writing as Kelsey Day
She's Not Broken
Concussive

About the Author

Sandy Lender is an international best-selling poet and award-winning author of fantasy, literary fiction, poetry, and short story work. She's a construction magazine editor by day and author of #GirlPower fantasy novels by night, living in Florida to help with sea turtle conservation and parrot rescue. You can follow her author page (Sandy Lender) on Amazon or subscribe to her author newsletter, SandySaysRead, to stay up to date. Visit her website for the subscription link at SandyLenderInk dot com.

With a four-year degree in English and thirty-year career in publishing, Sandy's successes include traditionally and self-published novels, hundreds of magazine articles, multiple short stories in competitive anthologies, a handful of technical writing awards, a handful of creative writing awards, and the 2023 Michael Knost Wings award.

Sandy's been writing stories since she was knee-high to a grasshopper when her great-grandmother shared her odd little tales of squeaky ghost-spiders around an apartment complex in Southern Illinois. The stories have developed to include strong young ladies working with dragons to save worlds from terrible fates, but those pesky spiders still show up from time to time.

There's always something brewing at Sandy Lender Ink headquarters where *some days, you just want the dragon to win.*

www.ingramcontent.com/pod-product-compliance
Lightning Source LLC
Chambersburg PA
CBHW051509260626

47162CB00008B/2889